The best
to my good
friend
Tim

William C. Moton

STORIES OF THE AFRICAN AMERICAN FRONTIER CALVARY

Buffalo Soldiers

WILLIAM C. MOTON

Order this book online at www.trafford.com
or email orders@trafford.com

Most Trafford titles are also available at major online book retailers.

Print information available on the last page.

ISBN: 978-1-4907-9557-7 (sc)
ISBN: 978-1-4907-9556-0 (hc)
ISBN: 978-1-4907-9555-3 (e)

Library of Congress Control Number: 2019907263

Trafford rev. 10/11/2019

www.trafford.com

North America & international
toll-free: 1 888 232 4444 (USA & Canada)
fax: 812 355 4082

This book is dedicated to my father, Glen Moton, and our family's helper for many years, Mrs. Rowena Bell—we called her MaReen. My father was born on a farm near Pelzer, Greenville County, South Carolina, in 1910. He was a WWII veteran who raised seven of us on his shoe repairman's salary and money from odd jobs. He always encouraged his children to study and get education he didn't have. During his lifetime, he met buffalo soldiers in their advanced years. Like most elderly, they told stories of their earlier lives.

MaReen was born in 1890 in the cotton country around Augusta, Georgia. She attended to the Moton children's needs when our parents worked. While doing so, she entertained us with stories of her youth.

The book was put together with the help of Ms. Lauren Mayet of Houma, Louisiana, a town in the bayou.

AUTHOR'S NOTE

This book contains stories of American unsung heroes. The mostly unknown and forgotten men who put their stamp on American history. The Ninth and Tenth US Cavalry and the Twenty-Fourth and Twenty-Fifth Infantry Regiments.

During the Indian Wars in the Southwest, these troops earned sixteen Congressional Medals of Honor. Their ranks were filled by men from the East, Midwest, and former slaves from the South. They were organized to relieve the hardships settlers faced along trails leading west. They built forts and roads, dams for rivers, and strung telegraph wires. Other duties were assisting peaceful Indians onto reservations and protecting railroad workers from Indian attacks while they laid tracks across the western plains. Their job required relentless pursuits of gunrunners, kidnapping Comancheros, and cattle rustlers. They brought federal law where none existed. They made long treks through the wide open spaces of Texas, New Mexico, Arizona, and Utah, eventually becoming known to Native Americans of the midwest and southern plains. These included Comanche, Cheyenne, Apache, Pawnee, Kickapoo, Ute, and Paiutes. Some were large nations, others small bands.

Those men, now faded memories, were neither heroes or, as some would claim from the comfort of their classrooms while giving opinions without facts, doups, forgetting that they lived in a different time and they did what those times dictated.

During the westward movement of settlers coming as far away as Europe, the troop known as Colored Troops made up one-fourth of all troops stationed on the frontier.

CHAPTER 1

When the Civil War ended, Joe Jr. was ten years old. He and a half dozen brothers and sisters were raised on a plantation in Arkansas and some of the only slaves who had both parents. During the war, the family had been sold to a family in Northeast Texas. He had been too young to do anything without supervision. He helped his mother and father gather cotton and put it into the long sacks that were dragged through the fields. The harvest would then be baled and kept in warehouses where cotton brokers would come and purchase them. The process was continuous. When war came, a blockade was put and enforced around Galveston Island, where it was usually shipped to England, France, and other countries where mills openly welcomed it. Some were smuggled into Mexico, where it found a market. When slavery ended, Texas slaves were the last to know. June 19 was declared the day of jubilee. A new struggle soon began. The family headed to a boomtown in East Texas. During those days, Texas had the same problem as the rest of the South. Their economy had been devastated. The status of the wealthy land and slave owner had ended. The former ruling class, without wealth, were the same as the poorer who had little to lose in the first place. What differed them was culture and education. Things were the same everywhere. Soon, good fortunes and faith dealt them a better hand. During the war, millions of domesticated cattle wandered and mixed with herds of longhorn that had been brought into the territory by the Spanish centuries earlier. This unique situation gave people the ability to round up and brand the roaming multitudes, providing a future for some to become big cattle owners and the new rich. The drovers and cowboys who worked the herds had a hand in the economy that exploded.

Joe Sr., like many ex-slaves, became an astute houseman and cowboy who worked the range gathering animals for long drives to railroads and stockyard on the other side of Indian territory. During those days, Joe Jr. did what his parents wanted—he got an education. During free time, he and his friends became good horse handlers. He yearned to follow the trails like his father. The urge was channeled by occupying his time riding the surrounding foothills with friends. Local whites steamed, thinking they were the last considered of society. They fumed at being manipulated by carpetbaggers and cunning, accommodating scalawags who controlled local politics. Those sentiments led to explosive encounters. They considered themselves victims of groups and agencies that helped the freed men. During the 1870s, Reconstruction was in effect. Colored Troops were stationed all over the South. The former Rebs were insulted by the presence of African American troops. Joe Jr. became aware of, ones stationed in the neighboring state, Kansas. He went to Fort Leavenworth and joined. He was seventeen but claimed to be older. It was hard to establish the age of those born during slavery. Most recruits had been field hands and laborers with limited education. With schooling and the ability to handle horses, Joe made an impression. At that age, being tall, pleasant, and intelligent, he began to receive promotions. He was later assigned to guarding the railroad being built close by. One day on the Kansas prairie, the sun was hot and promised to get hotter. Railroad tracks were being laid. The men were tough; the Irish foreman was tougher. Most track layers were immigrants who recently arrived from Europe; others were drifters from all over. The work was monotonous, grueling, and relentless. When breaks were taken, they were short. Then the routine continued with the heavy steel. When nights finally came, they returned to little camps built as they traveled. Some would wash, eat, and then fall into their little cots and sleep till the next morning. Seeking distractions, others would drink and gamble; others would just drink. Many sent their meager earnings to families back east or down south. Ones with passion, lust, and unspent energy spent their little money for a few minutes' romp with soiled doves.

Doves followed the tracks as relentlessly as the workers. Bordellos in mobile tents were forever present. A few of them worked solo because of unforeseen problems; most had pimps.

One day, he was patrolling as usual. The Ninth Colored Cavalry at the site were approached by a white troop on patrol. Their officer's name was Lieutenant Smith. The Ninth had a white lieutenant named Wolf. He, like his men, didn't have much experience. In those days, all the black troops' regiments had white officers. Many were proud of their commands. Others among them, such as the famous General Custer, who was downgraded to lieutenant colonel, did not want a black command. Captain Benteen of the Seventh Regiment also refused an Afro command. Both became immortalized later at the Battle of the Little Bighorn with the Sioux. The white patrol approached. Lieutenant Wolfe asked Corporal Joe to accompany him. He was the senior noncom with experience. Their sergeant was on another patrol.

The patrol arrived. The officers saluted one another. Joe Mounted stayed near. Lieutenant Smith said, "We are going to the Cheyenne village up ahead. Do you know it?"

Wolfe answered, "Yes, the one you are going to is pretty big. I hope you are not planning hostile actions against them. They are not friendly but haven't been violent in a while. We go there peacefully to eat buffalo sometimes as a sign of goodwill. They know the herds are getting scarce."

Lieutenant Smith said, "I'm going after some horse thieves. I advise you not to be belligerent. You don't have enough men to back you. Didn't your commanding office tell you that?"

"I knew about the stolen horses and figured the culpits were long gone."

"Then who told you about that particular village?"

He pointed to his Pawnee scout then beckoned him forward.

Lieutenant Wolfe said, "I don't speak their language, do you?"

"No, I was told by some Indians who hang around the fort."

Fort Indians hang around and would invent anything for a meal.

"Let corporal here talk to him. He can translate."

Joe, still close, began speaking in the Pawnee's language while using sign language. He finished and told the two officers. The scout told the lieutenant not to take the fort Indian's word. He was part of the patrol because he didn't like Cheyennes and wanted some of their scalps.

Lieutenant Wolfe told the other officer, "I will advise you to be very careful. That village is like a beehive. Don't disrespect them."

"Don't worry. I have been out west a year. I was trained before I came on how to deal with the savages."

They saluted. The patrol road off. The lieutenant's attitude was similar to many young officers arriving in the west who wanted to be known as aggressive. In the last years, the Cheyenne had witnessed several defeats. The power of repeating rifles had decimated their ranks during battles with the army. A few years earlier, a surveying company with buffalo soldiers as guards were attacked by many of them. The group took refuge on Beecher Island, a small wooded piece of land in the middle of a shallow stream. There, they held off repeated attacks for several days. One of their famous chiefs, Roman Nose, was killed. Two days had passed since the patrol passed.

Lieutenant Smith had continued toward the Cheyenne village. Lieutenant Wolfe's patrol continued to ride back and forth, guarding surroundings and the work crew. A lone rider appeared on the horizon, approaching on horseback. The Pawnee scout stopped in from of Joe Jr., knowing he was the only one who could communicate with him.

Showing exhaustion, he began to tell of the recent tragedy with sign language and a little English thrown in, "When we went to the village, all the people came from their dwellings. The lieutenant couldn't speak their language and told me to tell the reason we were there.

"We are enemies, but I speak their language. When I told them about the thief and we came for some of their Braves. They became agitated. The chief asked why, out of all the people on the plains, we came to them. The Braves and women laughed. I told the lieutenant what he said. He told me to tell the chief a reputable source gave them the information. The chief said, 'Bring the person. He can tell him who the Braves are.' The lieutenant excitedly told him to tell the chief he was lying. 'I was not a fool to tell him that.' When I refused, the lieutenant pulled his pistol and shouted, 'I am a representative of the US government! I want that man!' One of the Braves excitedly talked to the chief. The lieutenant didn't understand. The man explaining to the chief—he should have listened to avoid trouble. Not understanding the man was trying to help the situation, he shot him.

"The Braves were armed. The chief shouted shooting began. The lieutenant fell first. Others fell from their mounts. As I looked around, only me and a few soldiers were left. The Braves who had taken cover rushed toward us. Me and the remaining soldiers galloped away under heavy fire. I did not get none of their scalps. They did not get mine."

Lieutenant Wolfe had thirty men under his command. He told the company representative what happened. The representative told him his job was to guard the train and crew. The lieutenant was adamant that he would return in two days. Out of the thirty, he would take twelve. The rest would stay. Soldiers could not leave others in the field without investigating. He assembled the soldiers he had chosen and left with the scout. The lieutenant and his men had the Cheyenne's respect the same as with other red men on the plains. They did not unnecessarily engage them and gave a helping hand when they could. The older ones had been in the South as slaves when some of the tribes there had black slaves.

The patrol approached large boulders of rocks covered by trees and lots of scrub grass. They heard a faint cry, "Help, help me. Please help me!"

They quickened their pace till they were closer, then the head of a soldier poked from cover. Visibly shaken, he began talking, "Thank God, it's you, not them devils. Me and Frank got away, the only survivors."

He pointed to the scout. "He took off. Me and Frank rode like the wind till his horse stumbled. He was able to jump. We ran into these rocks. They didn't come close, but bullets were flying. We banged away at them as much as we could and kept the varmints at bay. They hung in the open until one dropped. The others, seeing we had good cover, rode away. Frank died. A bullet had struck him. We didn't have time to try and stop the blood. Since then, I've been scared almost to death but hoping and praying they didn't return with a whole bunch."

The lieutenant told him, "Stay here till we return. First, let's get the soldier buried so the critters don't get him."

They arrived at an abandoned village. Even the poles that held the tepees had been taken. The bodies of the soldiers lay where they had fallen. Two horses were close by. The other is Indians had taken to either trade or (when buffalo and other is animals they hunted were scarce) to eat. Looking around and seeing no survivors, the lieutenant told the men to dig a mass grave for the bodies. Soldiers from the fort would rebury them later.

To the surprise of many, but not some, the bodies had not been mutilated, a common custom each tribe practiced. The Cheyenne, knowing the soldiers would take revenge if it happened to them, had forgone the practice. One who lay with his mouth wide, tongue cut out, and ears cut off was easy to recognize. It was Lieutenant Smith. The Plains Indians had different but similar beliefs. The lieutenant would arrive in the afterlife called the happy hunting ground handicapped and not able to talk or hear. A closer look saw that his eyes were closed and singed. He would also be blind. When the burials were finished, they took off to pick up the lone survivors left in the rocks.

They were traveling at a steady pace when there was a sudden change in the weather. The wind seemed hotter. Birds began passing overhead in droves. Then it seemed the ground began to move, crickets and bugs flew past, then reality struck. The surroundings were filled with the smallest of creatures crawling, jumping, or hopping. Snakes slithered along with hopping rabbits and groundhogs.

The lieutenant said, "Corporal, something's happening."

They were riding in a low area, galloping to the summit. They could smell what they saw—a fast-moving prairie fire coming their way, burning everything in its path. Joe told the lieutenant. "Sir, I suggest we make tracks."

The lieutenant held his hand up. "Let's move."

They broke into a gallop. Larger animals—dear, antelope, and others—ran with their natural enemies—coyotes, wild pigs, cows, and bulls. All ran to escape the oncoming inferno. The men slapped their mounts to make them run faster. The horses, with their instincts alerted and awareness of impending doom, needed little encouragement. The ferocity and unbridled fury destroying everything in its path drove them on.

Joe shouted, "Sir, do you remember the ravine we passed coming this way with a stream running alongside it?"

"Sure, corporal."

"I have an idea, sir."

"We take cover at that drop. We run into the stream with the horses to get everything wet, especially the blankets. Then we run back to the league, cover ourselves and the horses with the soaked blankets, and wait. With luck, the fire will jump the ravine to reach vegetation on the other side then continue until it burns itself out. The stream will slow it."

The men huffed, puffed, and rode at top speed. They reached the ravine and followed the plan. After the ferocious heat passed, they slowly stood.

A man asked, "Y'all feel that?"

They stood with their hands out. It had begun to drizzle. Another man, full of awe, asked, "Can you believe? It's raining in a place it never rains."

Joe said, "Y'all prays musta been hard as mine. 'Cause they was sure answered."

It rained harder. They jumped around in it and were joined by the lieutenant. They arrived at the railroad camp before sunset. The representative of operations said, "Welcome back. Coming from that direction, you fellows musta had a lot of luck or missed that fire because, of course, you wouldn't be here. We are grateful for architects and engineers who did their inventions well. A project of this magnitude could not have been taken without forethought and investigations. See, there is no high grass around either side. A firestorm would never get enough fuel to develop and build pluse. The red devils cannot hide anywhere without being seen.

CHAPTER 2

Late afternoon in the Texas Panhandle, a stage traveled quickly along a lonely road. Inside rode the famous civil war hero, General William Tecumseh Sherman, with his adjutant and two other officers. He said, "Those brunettes should have arrived by now."

The adjutant replied, "Escorts are sometimes late. This is still hostile territory."

"Of course! That's the reason for the meeting we are going to attend. It is very important," the general said. "The meeting will end either one way or the other. The head man or chief who keeps things riled up will be pacified or we will use other options. Either will happen soon."

The general was famous for dealing harshly with adversaries. During the war, he burned through the South to the sea. Famous cities burned: Atlanta and Savannah in Georgia then Charleston and other cities in the Carolinas. A large mob of unruly low-class men named Bummers followed in his wake, pillaging and burning plantations and large and small farms along the way.

The general continued, "They will come around like the Comanches after losing their ability to sustain themselves. They fought one another like the tribes in Europe, Africa, and Asia did before and some still do. In the end, the strongest always wins. Like the naturalist said."

The adjutant spoke, "Charles Darwin."

"That's right," the general confirmed. "Our people and government are the strongest tribe around. We are on the side of history. Our destiny has been manifested. We have fought a long war. With God's help, we will evolve from seas to the oceans. The law of the tomahawk, war-clad battle lance, and lynch rope is to end. From now, it's going to be law, law and order. Arriving Anglos and other immigrants will adapt. Who knows if the heathens will. Sherman along with General Sheridan the famous! The only good Indian is a dead one."

Had wanted to hang Geronimo, Nana, and other Chiricahua Apache leaders. Other generals intervened. One of the officers looked toward the horizon.

"General, look."

The general was surprised to see a large group of Indians on a distant hill. He banged on the inside roof. "Yey, up there, look at that hill."

The driver heard, looked, and saw Indians slowly descending the hill. He shouted, "Yes, sir! I see them!" He cracked his whip. "Ya, ya, ya, get up, you critters."

The coach sped up. The guard said, "I'm as ready as I'm gonna be."

The driver suddenly saw a cloud of dust. "Somebody is coming this way!" he hollered. "I hope it's not more of them."

The general looked out the window. The other officers looked out the other. The adjutant shouted, "General, I think that's our escort!"

The headquarters in Fort Sill, Oklahoma, was busy. It had taken a few days to arrange and meet with the chiefs and their entourage. The general finished negotiating the future of the Kiowa nation through an interpreter. The group then left. The general wiped his brow. "Wow, I'm glad that's over. Dealing with them is like dealing with the devil."

The officers and noncoms standing around laughed.

The general continued, "Keep those doors open and let out some of that hell heat they brought. Mind you, I am a bit sympathetic. It's understandable they want the best deal they can for their people's future."

This wasn't the first time the Kiowa were called devils. In the mid-1860s during the Civil War, the Texas frontier was left unguarded. Many of the state's troops and citizens left to go east and fight for the Confederate cause. The Kiowa and Comanches, emboldened by their departures, rampaged, killing, burning, and plundering across the countryside. During one of those episodes, they kidnapped a group of settlers/families. Some of the women they took as wives. One of the settlers was an ex-slave, Britton Johnson.

The Kiowa dubbed Black Fox for his cleverness, had a family taken. After a hand-to-hand fight with one of their principal warriors, Britt won. He negotiated a deal. The settlers gave a large herd of horses in exchange for the hostages, including the women taken as wives. His family stayed awhile and was adopted into the tribe. Later, they returned to the settlement and resumed their lives.

The general continued, "Tomorrow, the colonel will attend to other problems. My major informed me he has a man in his regiment who was with you when you campaigned in the South with me."

"I think he meant he followed you, sir. The man is adamant he was there!"

General Sherman had military jurisdiction from the Appalachians to the Mississippi River. Fifty thousand slaves had been left in Georgia whom he could have helped but didn't. He, like many Union officers of his time, disliked the freedmen. They helped free them from the plantations but had no idea they were going to be part of postwar society. For some, freedom for them was unthinkable. A special order was known Special Field Order No. 15, forty acres were to be set aside for free Negroes who headed households. Twenty thousand acres of occupied land were vacated by fleeing white owners. When the war ended, the same whites returned and challenged the freedmen as squatters. Under the administration after President Lincoln's assassination, Andrew Johnson, the new president, a Southern Democrat sympathizer. The challenge was accepted. The freedmen were left helpless. The general in charge reneged on his promise. His feelings were open but not formally expressed and, in public, toned down. Expressions by the military had become accommodative. They dubbed colored military brunettes. In a few years, those brunettes would supply up to a third of all troopers on the frontier, cavalry or infantry. The senior military understood, regardless of their individual feelings. Blacks had been part of all campaigns since colonial time and, in the future, would probably account for a large portion of needed manpower as teamsters or in other functions that helped in war efforts and combat troops. These were undisputed facts before large-scale immigration from Europe to feed growing demands of labor. The industrial might of the growing US was gaining strength and being felt on the world's economic stage of competition. Colored troops would take advantage of opportunities offered; personal advancement would follow.

The general asked, "Who is this soldier?"

He was told, "Sergeant Craves of the Tenth, a brunette."

"I would like to speak to him. I don't want to bother you with trivial nonsense," the colonel said.

"That's nonsense. I would like nothing better than to see someone from the past. It's been almost eight years."

"He's on the parade ground, drilling men," the colonel explained.

"Don't matter, bring him."

A moment later, the general was seated with the other officers. Craves came in and stood at attention. The colonel and major were with him.

"Pardon, sir, the man's here." The major motioned Craves forward. He strutted to attention, saluted, and stood. The general casually returned one but remained seated.

The major said, "The sergeant was part of your escort the other day."

"Oh, so you were one of the men who saved our hair?" The officers around laughed. "You were with me during the war, they tell me."

"Yes, sir, me and a bunch of hands had just left the plantation when y'all came. We were glad to follow y'all, and we were there when that burning stuff was going on. I was young like some of the others. We helped doing what we could. We didn't do none of that burning, but we helped in other ways."

The general said, "Many refugees became stevedores. I see what a fine fellow you turned out to be. You were a boy then, you are a man now. A sergeant no less." He stood and held out his hand to be shaken. They finished. The other officers had stood. The general saluted. It was returned. "I salute you again." He looked at the officers. "Who did the same. Glad you joined us, Sergeant Craves."

When formalities finished, Craves left.

Two regiments stood in front of the headquarters building. One by a river was black, the other white. Their commander, Col. Reginald Mackenzie, was on leave.

The river stood beside a large Kiowa village with over a thousand inhabitants. The men stood at attention in their particular groups. Sergeant Craves was in one.

A group of cannons in full view were pointed across the river at the camp. Its occupants could clearly see. The day was hot in most parts of the Southwest from the Mississippi River to the Pacific. The land was sunbaked. The winter nights were extremely cold in the mountains and had relief during the day.

The colonel addressed the assemblage, "Men, recently the Kiowa have done what they never did, at least in good fate. They agreed to be assigned a reservation in Indian Country, where other tribes, large and small, have established homes for the last forty years. Everybody knows they are proud people. They accepted the offer like others of their race and want to thrive. With our help, they will. Unfortunately, some time when groups parlay to work out their differences, things happened to interfere with the process. In this instance, one of their sub-chiefs has been identified as the culprit in the slaughter of an immigrant family who were traveling peacefully. This afternoon, soldiers from both regiments will cross the river to the encampment. There will be fifty, including negotiators and translators. The Indians under our command would be offensive to the Kiowa because of tribal differences and will not go."

The fifty crossed the river; a major was in charge. "They know why we are here. There will be no hostile movement on our part. They want to protect the sub-chief and will argue. We were at war when the assault happened. I don't know how they think the court will judge a man or men who murdered and mutilate a lone family, war or no war."

Arriving by boat on the village side of the river, they were met by a large group of onlookers. Children playing stopped to watch then followed them.

Entering, they were met by growling guard dogs that barked to announce their presence then growled as they followed. The troops walked to the center then stood. The major walked in front of the chief who stood with an unsmiling face with arms crossed. The translator, standing beside the major, began delivering words to the chief.

"I am here to inform you that progress is being made to assign you to an area where your people will be protected and taken care of. In the future, you, like other tribes, will learn farming and animal raising for your existence. This is the way of the white men and other people who live good. No longer will you roam looking for food to feed yourselves. Accept our ways and you will be well fed and, I hope, happy. Food and provisions will be dispersed and distributed to your people to help your transition. A representative of the government will be assigned to help you."

The translator, using words and signs, relayed the message. "The major continued on this occasion and brings a message for mutual cooperation. I am here also to apprehend the man who murdered a family."

When the translator finished, a group of warriors chambered bullets into their Winchesters, getting them ready to fire. The soldiers did the same. The chief, hearing the reaction, raised his hand, turned to his men, and spoke. The warriors looked stoically ahead.

"Wait. There is no reason for blood," the major said. "Big guns on the other side of the river can fire into your village. Women and children and old people will die. The one responsible should come forward and avoid suffering for his people. Men do such things, cowards don't."

When the translator finished, mumbling came from the warriors. Then one of them slowly walked through a corridor made between them with a rifle in his hand. He stopped in front of the major and presented it. Then he said in limited English, "Man you look for no coward, I man."

Noncommissioned officers surrounded him. The officer walked away; the con-cons followed with the prisoner.

Sergeant Craves's duties continued at Fort Sill. His job required he work with black Seminole Indian scouts. One of them had an attractive daughter of marriageable age. He moved in with her and began a relation. Like many couples at the time, they lived without the benefit of a formal marriage. He soon learned the local Indian dialect. The woman's father was a former runaway from Cherokees in South Carolina. He was full black. Her mother was half Creek and black. They had met during a war with US soldiers and marines who invaded Florida to pacify the Seminoles. The army wanted to return who they called runaway swamp niggers to their former owners in the Carolinas and Georgia. The blacks who adapted to the harsh environment of the Everglades stayed. Two young men adopted by the parents of Craves's woman had been brought as slaves of the Cherokee to Oklahoma territory.

The Cherokee and other tribes had been exiled from their homelands in the Southeastern states. During the Civil War, those tribes split and joined warring factions. Years earlier, slaves had gone on a rampaged. Some escaped and were eventually caught while running to freedom in Mexico. Mexico abolished slavery when they got their freedom from Spain in 1821. During the rebellion, one slave had been especially ferocious. The Cherokees named him Tecumseh after the Shawnee chief who had fought to keep whites out of his land in Ohio. Tecumseh they no longer wanted anything to do with. The other had taken the name Cherokee because the name given to him was hard to pronounce. He used the name for so many years; he became fond of it and continued using it. Their fathers were both Cherokee. Their mixed mothers spoke little English. When the war was over, ex-slaves, along with their host, became scouts for the military. When Tecumseh and Cherokee were out of their teens, they joined the black regiments.

The sergeant received orders West to another assignment. The young men, being adventurous, joined him. He asked permission to take the woman along and was told that since they were not legal, it was up to her. Her mother thought the West was still wild and was afraid of the unknown for her daughter. Shedina didn't want to leave her mother.

Sergeant Craves, former slave and field hand, stevedore on New Orleans docks, experienced at training recruits and guarding stages' lives from bandits and hostile Indians was off to new horizons in the far West, accompanied by two young men raised by Indians who spoke little English.

CHAPTER 3

It was a full moon on a star-filled night. Darkness was beginning to give way to the slow-appearing light of dawn. A patrol of the Tenth US Cavalry were dismounted, resting their horses. A lone rider approached at a fast gallop. Arriving, he made hand signs to a sergeant who used signs to do the same. The arriving man was an Apache scout dressed in regular Indian clothing. The Sergeant Jenkins Cravis was in charge of the patrol. Corporal Joe Jr. was second in command. Privates Tecumseh and Cherokee were there.

They were on the trail of a gang of deadly scalp hunters who also kidnapped children to sell across the border. They mounted their horses and rode away at a gallop. Later, they dismounted and walked the horses in single file. It was believed the eight held four settlers and a few Indian children. The Indians had survived a massacre of their parents. Arriving close to the camp, the sergeant told a soldier as he was leaving, "Try to get a count of them."

Twelve soldiers left their horses guarded by one of them and followed the sergeant with pistols dawn. There was no campfire. The men were clever enough to know a fire could be seen a long distance in open desert. The man returned. "There is one guard." A breeze that had blown through the night was subsiding. The sun on the horizon promised to bring unbearable heat as the day progressed. The land was absent of vegetation except for large and small cacti of various kinds with dangerous needles the men knew to be careful of. Arriving, they saw the hostages tied in small groups. The bandits slept scattered. Sergeant Craves, with signs, told four of his men to guard the children. The others looked to get a drop on the unsuspecting men by slowly creeping. One of them awakened, fired his pistol, and hallowed visitors. The others scrambled to their feet, guns drawn. Looking around, they fired without seeing anything. Men in their situation slept ready for emergencies.

The soldiers charged, shooting. The captured children screamed and wiggled. Tied up, there was little they could do. The bandits fled to their horses. Each saddled his and covered the others. They rode off, shouting orders to one another. Two soldiers guarding the children had received slight wounds. Looking, they discovered four Indian children.

The sergeant said, "Lucky they didn't bother that older girl. She looks about sixteen."

Another said, "With those lowlifes, the little ones were lucky to escape. They would have been used property. Worthless."

"Virgins bring more money. It's good we rescued them in time. That might not have stopped them."

Too long. They walked through the camp, seeing what was left, and attended the wounded. All the hostages had survived. The scout questioned the Indian children.

"We were right. The adults were killed and scalped. Children's are worthless. Alive, they are worth something as slaves. They are alive because they are used to hardships," one of the soldiers said.

"I don't see nothing wrong with them. They are scared and need baths. That's all"

Joe Jr. said, "I think I saw a couple of them in town."

The sergeant said, "The German people won't be hard to find. They are some of the immigrants who came a couple of months ago. We'll find out about the Indians when we pass that village on the way back to the fort."

Traveling in stifling heat, they heard gunfire in the distance. Picking up their pace, they arrived at the scene.

Six painted Indians were circling a small farmhouse on horses. One was trying to open the corral to get the horses. Two with rifles fired repeatedly at the house. The others used bows and flaming arrows. The house had been struck. It was flaming. A cow close by laid dead; arrows protruded from its side. A dog nearby was also dead. A donkey could be heard banging and kicking the inside of the barn nearby. A repeating rifle protruded from a window shot barrages of withering fire, when it withdrew another appeared and continued spraying bullets. The patrol acted quickly and entered the melee. The surprised Indians, after a moment, were reduced by two. The rest rode off. The sergeant, corporal, and a private dismounted and walked toward the house. The sergeant turned and said, "The rest of you dismount and rest."

The group continued to the house. A door opened. A black woman stepped out, holding a rifle while two small children clung to her wide dress. The boy was about ten. The girl about 6. The woman, Barbara Johnson, was medium built, dark, and attractive. Her features showed she had lived a difficult life. her family were resent arrives.

She stepped back so the men could enter. They were surprised to see a black man lying facedown in a pool of blood that ran from wounds in his back. Two other children stood by. One was a girl about three. The other almost grown and held a rifle. The woman, with teary eyes, knelt and caressed the back of her man's head. "Poor John," she sobbed. The children joined her in the outburst of emotion. The sarge knelt close. He immediately recognized John Johnson. He had stopped and spoken to the man several times in town when the family came to get supplies. The man, was dead. His wife, continued sobbing, "Oh lord, my god, oh god. He's gone. He's gone. Oh, my poor children's father is gone. He always said better days were coming. He'd smile and say, 'I hope they hurry.' All these years and he end up like this."

The sarge stood and helped her rise. She leaned on his chest, sobbing. He patted her back. "Those Germans moved close to town and built a settlement. Some did, like us, build homesteads. A lot of them came in the same wagon train with us all the way from St. Louis. Other people who spoke a funny language came too. All this time, the Indians had been friendly. They'd stop, and water their horses themselves. Something musta ticked them off."

The sarge said, "They are a different band." He continued, "We will bury him and put the Indians in a common grave so buzzards and coyotes don't get them. We have children we rescued from kidnappers and are on our way to the Fort. You and the children better come along. The whole territory is in unrest. Nowhere is safe. Gather things that are not heavy. We have packhorses for your wagon. Bring it in front and bring that donkey in the barn we heard."

"I have a little money I saved from the vegetables we sell in town. I also have these." She walked a few steps and picked a small tin box from a drawer in a corner cabinet. She opened it and showed him.

The sarge picked up two. "Ham silver nuggets."

She said, "An old man gave them and that donkey to us. He was passing. We let him eat. He was kind of weak and sick with fever. It wasn't cold. So we fixed a place for him in the barn. We fed him soup and hot meals. When he got better, he left those things, then rode off on another donkey. He came with two."

The soldiers leaned on their shovels. Barbara put things into the horse-dawn wagons. Her children helped. When things were ready, they rode off. When it was getting dark, they turned onto a road where a group of Indians came from cover behind large rocks and surrounded them. After a discussion, the scout explained it was better that the group remained. The sergeant, scout, Indian children, and a few soldiers would go into the village and explain everything. This was because they were on alert. Hostiles left another reservation and went on a killing and burning spree. In the past, when that happened, townspeople would organize retaliate and kill any Indian—man, woman, or child. The most famous had been at Sand Creek in Colorado territory. Further north, a Cheyenne village had been attacked by cavalry. Hundreds of the tribe had been slandered. Their chief, Black Kettle, and his wife's tent flew American flags. He had government papers saying his people were not to be molested. Deaths like those were repeated if soldiers, scouts, along with a few Indian guards, arrived at the village with the children. It was large with many dwellings. Nearby, harvested cornstalks stood as evidence of the locals' work. A small herd of sheep grazed nearby. A well had been dug to provide water. The sarge estimated at least three hundred adults, not including old people. Adding the children, there were about a thousand inhabitants on a reservation with their movement restricted. Hunting animals was allowed but they were scarce in this area. Buffalo, deer, and antelope were plentiful to Plains Indians. A few states had the last of them. These people had been told to live off crops they produced. Arizona and New Mexico, being arid, receive little rain, and half is covered with near deserts or deserts. The government was to supplement their diets with federal of beef and flour. Before the peace, they raided the local territory, and in Mexico, Haciendas.

There had been numerous battles in Mexican states along the border. The government of Sonora had offered a bounty for Apache scalps. There was a price for men's and different prices for women's and children's. Now scalp-hunting parties roamed, looking to enrich themselves. All Native American hair was the same texture. They were all in danger. Rewards were being paid to lowlifes who collected the grisly trophies. Defiant chiefs fought the Mexicans and Americans who chased and killed them. Americans were mostly hated for building permanent housing and fencing land. After many of their famous chiefs had died or were killed, they pessimistically and begrudgingly but pragmatically accepted peace.

When the group entered the village, a middle-aged chief welcomed them. Other inhabitants curiously followed to see what happened. The chief was agreeable. The children were not his people but they could stay. Then he began to complained through the scout who interpreted their rations were short and, when received, were sometimes foul with varmint. He said, "Tell the major at the fort that no one would eat such food. The suppliers are stealing everything and enriching themselves."

Craves told him about the attack on the homestead. He responded none of his people were reasonable. Craves told how they were after scalp hunters who doged his people. He was told that added to the hostile is feelings. Many young men left the village to roam, pillage, burn, and kill in retaliation with the renegades. He explained they should come close to the village and. The group should remain with them tonight. That way, they would not be ambushed along the road at night.

The small group, soldiers, the German, Indian, children, and Barbara Anna's family, entered the village. They were invited to an open shelter in the middle of the village so they could be guarded.

After a meal, the children followed the Indian children to watch them play. The Indian children looked with curiosity at the Germans' blond hair and the coarse hair of Barbara's children. They were also curious about their skin color. The women gathered around Barbara Ann and curiously inspected her. The men formed a group and watched the Indians do their style of arm wrestling and flips. Finishing, they threw knives and showed off their skills at knife fighting. The soldiers trained in hand-to-hand combat and anything-goes rough-and-tumble styles, since childhood showed theirs. Each learned the advantages of the other. The night passed; everyone slept.

The next day, they resumed their travel. Morning turned into midday; the sun burned from a cloudless sky. They stayed in open ground, making sure they couldn't be ambushed. The soldiers were spread out to protect the civilians traveling between them while riding. Craves told Barbara, who held the rein to the horses as they pulled the wagon. "The donkey, tied to the wagon, trotted along." Craves said, "The weight is off the horses. It's good to travel relaxed," he said.

Two young children were with her. Her oldest daughter rode on a horse alongside the eldest German girl. The others rode double satting in front of the soldiers. The scout rode in the lead. Corporal Joe covered the rear. All seemed normal. Suddenly, Joe yelled to the men ahead, "Tell the sarge we have company! I saw a bright flash coming from that hill! I'm sure it's medal being used to communicate with someone."

Craves got the message and rode close to Barbara. "This is where we do what I discussed."

She quickly grabbed the small girl and put her on one of the saddled horses alongside the wagon then swung up behind her child. "We gonna ride, so hang on."

Craves grabbed the small boy and did the same. The older girl did the same with a child. The Indian came into view on the ridge. Seeing the party arranging to run then attacked. Shots rang out, the reorganized party galloped off, leaving the wagon and donkey. Soldiers fired shots knowing they were too distant to be effective but giving notice, getting close would be dangerous. They turned onto another road to avoid a trap in case someone was waiting ahead. Joe hollered, "We still have away to go to. Maintain our distance. Our horses are good for endurance. Their ponies are fast at sprints and will soon tire."

A group stopped and fired a barrage. Some of the pursuers fell from their mounts. Others returned fire and followed. Craves hollered, "We can't continue this pace! There is an outcropping ahead. Let's make it to the high ground. In the open air, the shots will be heard for miles."

They reached the outcropping. The group dismounted, huffing, puffing, and pulling the horse behind. Exhausted, they reached high ground. Bullets rang, panged, and ricocheted all around. The children, crying in fear, all hurried for cover mostly behind rocks. The renegades stopped below. Without cover, they rode in circles to avoid the barrage coming from skilled troops.

After a spell, the painted leader hollered, making exaggerated movements to the rocks alone with arm and hands that easily could be interpreted as curses. He finished and trotted away, followed by his men.

Craves said, "I guess they had enough and don't want to lose more men."

The corporal said, "I guess they will have donkey meat tonight."

The tired group were happy to see them leave. They rested and looked one another over for wounds, they drank water, rubbed the horses, and watered them then, rested and continued their journey. Before reaching the fort, they heard a bugle blow and were soon met by a soldier escort.

By midafternoon, they reached the fort and were greeted by soldiers and the garrison commander, a major named Gallinger. He said, "I sent the patrol, thinking some settlers were under attack. See you got those German kids."

Looking on, he saw the black family. "That's John Johnson's family. Where is he?"

"Renegades got him. He's buried at his place."

The major continued, "Those Germans won't have to go far some are at a tent city they built while you were absent. They are afraid of the roaming bands of white and red renegades. One hunts scalps for money, the other just hunts scalps. That was some rescue. I'm gonna make sure you men are remembered for your outstanding job."

That evening, the men relaxed in one of their barracks. Four played cards. Others stood or sat conversing. Tecumseh stood, watching a man move cards around, challenging them to tell which card the pea was under. After the soldiers playing failed, he stood and held up a coin. "Oh, the dealer said I take money from men who can speak English and find the pea."

Everyone stood and watched as the half-Indian held his chin with one hand as if in thought. After a few moments, he pointed to the man's hand. The man acted dumb. Everyone watched. Tecumseh grabbed the man's hand and squeezed. The pea fell from it. Everybody rose and shouted, wanting their money returned. Man mumbled, "Dirty half-breed."

A private named Abraham said, "All them foreigners coming to settle on Indian land. Why the government letting them do it?"

Private Willis said, "I ain't going to try and figure the government's reason for what they do. They been good to us so far. And as far as I can see, this whole country going to change. We here to help keep the peace. The Indian done roamed this country since who knows when. They gonna have to start farming like everybody. Where them foreigners came from, they couldn't own land. Only blue blood had it, people worked for them."

Abraham laughed. "Blue blood. Y'all heard that? Ain't nobody got no blue blood."

He was joined by a group who patted their thighs and laughed, catching their breath. "Man, blue blood. Who ever heard of such nonsense."

The private spoke up. "No, their blood ain't blue. They call the royalty that. You know, counts, dukes, lords, them folks. Another reason is them blue blood related, but they always war with one another. Counts fight counts, dukes fight dukes. They have armies that kill thousands, just like the war we just had. Thing is, over there, it happens all the time. They had an emperor named Napoleon, who went conquering and killing all over the place. They even have a group called viceroys, earls, and a bunch of names I don't understand. But like Willis said, the Indians gonna have to learn like we did back yonder. Work the fields."

A soldier sitting on his bunk said, "I just finished reading a letter I got from my sister. The federal soldiers are starting to leave the South. I was a soldier down there after the war." He shook his head. "It's going to be a whole bunch of trouble. White folks ain't changed. They ain't forgot the old days and them ways they gonna try to change it back. We suppose to be helping guarding the Indians and the people in town. Them town people are a lot better than the ones back yonder, but they don't give a spit about us, and I don't give a spit about them. Before I joined the outfit, all I ever saw was the backside of a mule farting and crapping while I pushed a plow through the field. Now we done fought, the hostiles, killed some. They done killed a bunch of us. Now I'm thinking about leaving this Indian stuff and going back and helping the folks."

Corporal Joe, sitting on a bunk, said, "Things are changing all over. Just think, one of the territories trying to be a state has women voting. I think it's called Wyoming. I was close to there when I guarded the railroad workers. They were mostly Irish and German. They worked from sun up to sun down laying tracks. Shucks, they didn't make no more money than us. We just had to watch curious Indians. Sometimes, they came to watch and wonder what new thing the white man had brought to their land."

The workers were afraid the onlookers would bother them. I'd think about the Chinese laying tracks coming from California to meet us. They came across the ocean and were getting less money than poor whites.

He ended the conversation. "I know something nobody never would think. There is a colored officer coming."

Men shaving stopped to listen. The card game stopped.

"Yeah, he's soon graduating West Point. They say he will be assigned out west. I hope he comes here—the chaplain who teaches us reading and writing is good but a regular line officer that will be something.

He continued, "I heard y'all talking about blue bloods. They say they gonna get rid of them. They been around since the beginning. I don't know how they gonna do that. Even in the Old Testament, they had kings to run the society. One of the books I been reading by a guy over in Germany about something called communism. Everybody is supposed to have the same things. They not gonna be no bosses. They have a lot of lazy people. I wonder how that's gonna work?"

The sarges standing in the corner with Tecumseh and Cherokee said, "I suggest all of you don't play cards with them they had colored mamas and Indian Daddies. Way back, some of y'all folks were slaves to Indians in the Carolinas, Georgia, Alabama, Mississippi and Louisiana. Half y'all got white or red man's blood running in y'all, so don't treat them funny 'cause they can't speak good English. Y'all sound like y'all just left the field."

What none of them knew was that blacks had mixed with the native population since arriving centuries before. Some were Powhatan, Pequots, Iroquois Potawatomi, and many others.

CHAPTER 4

The town of Winslow, Arizona, was not far from the Mexican border and had begun to thrive. The boomtown of Tombstone, where a silver strike had taken place, was close. It had a large Mexican and Chinese population and some blacks.

Tucson and Prescott, larger towns, had railroads stations and were developing. They beckoned families, storekeepers, and people who wanted to stop drifting for a while to build homes.

Barbara Ann walked out of the general store where everything was sold. Her younger daughter was talking to a little white girl her age. Barbara gave both a piece of candy. A moment later, the girl's father walked over, grabbed her hand, looked at Barbara's daughter, and said, "She ain't talking to you no more."

His daughter protested. "That's Annie-May, we were just talking."

The man said, "I don't want you talking to her kind no more. Give that candy back."

She obeyed and handed the candy to Barbara. Pulling his daughter, he brushed past the sergeant who was approaching. When he got close, he asked what was about.

"You know his kind. He don't get along with nobody."

In town, the man was known as Jeb the Reb. He scouted sometimes for patrols with white officers. He had been a scout for Major John Mosby, "the Gray Ghost," in Virginia who had led hit-and-run campaigns against union supplies during the war. Mosby's attacks had been successful until the wars ended. Jeb had come west and eventually taken the oath of allegiance. His experience with the Gray Ghost had earned him a reputation of being clever and sly. He had gotten into the good graces of some who shared his feeling and some who thought he was valuable.

The sarge walked with Barbara and her daughter. "I heard about your new job. I'm happy for you."

"Well, I'm just helping out. I lend a hand in cooking and cleaning. Since we left the place, there isn't much to do, we can't grow nothing where we staying. The money I get will help. Them children grow so fast I make dress after dress. And that boy busts his breeches faster than I can patch them." She laughed now. "He's got patches on top of patches. With the money, I'm gonna buy him some store-bought pants and, later, some shoes. He done got too old to go around barefoot."

"I don't want to make you late," he said. "I'll come over sometime. You still over there with the Germans, right?"

"Yeah, I got the children studying with their kids. They help them practice English. I guess they will learn everything together and don't have to worry about traveling to school."

"I better get going. Goodbye."

At the end of town, outside a saloon, a young Indian man named Chato talked to his sister who was close to his age. "The tribe don't approve of you and Morning Glory coming to town." He put his hands on her shoulders. She did likewise. They leaned, putting their heads together. "You are still my sister. I hope you well."

She turned and walked through the batwing entrance of the saloon, continuing inside to a table and sat with a woman her age with two black soldiers. Craves, at the bar, held hands with an attractive, overdressed, and well made-up black woman. Her name was Hazel. She smiled, laughed at something funny, playfully squeezed his nose then sexually gyrated her body. Looking over her shoulder, while walking away. The two soldiers continued talking to the women. The one who had come in was named Happyness. The women took turns going to the bar for drinks. On the other side of the room, the woman who had left Craves arrived to take orders from a group of gamblers. A fancily dressed black man pushed back from the table. Two white gamblers leaned forward to rake a pile of money toward them. The black man reached to his back, brought out a throwing knife, threw it into the air, caught it then stabbed the table close to the money then pulled a Derringer and cocked it.

"Y'all done come down to a colored place to gamble. Y'all done lost and think y'all going to buffalo me." Shaking his head, "Y'all wrong. Y'al all the wrong Georgia boy. This my place. Come back ready to win or lose or stay uptown."

The two gamblers picked the money in front of them up, left the remaining in the middle where the knife was sticking, then left the table. Pushing through the batwings to leave, they passed Corporal Joe, who rushed in, hurrying to the bar where Sergeant Craves was finishing a beer. He sat the glass on the bar and turned when hearing the excited voice. "Sergeant!"

Joe put his hand on his arm. "You won't believe this. Those dirty, no-good kidnappers are in town."

"I would have thought they were out of the territory by now," the sarge said.

"Maybe they didn't think we got a good look at them then maybe they don't care."

The men went to the sheriff's office and explained what had happened. The sheriff and all the townspeople knew about the kidnapping and the return of the children. No one had an idea who the culprits were. The sheriff, knowing the soldiers were out of their jurisdiction, told them both, "Follow me so there won't be a disturbance. You can back me in case of trouble."

It was midday when they entered the saloon. A few customers lingered at the bar, others at tables, drinking with a women or playing cards. One or two played solitaire. Two black men sat at a corner table. The trio approached the bar.

"Hold it right there," the bartender said. "We don't want soldiers here in uniform. When y'all show, trouble starts."

The sheriff said, "This is official. They are with me."

They continued a table where three men sat. Two were white; one was Mexican. One of the whites had a big scar running down one cheek. The Mexican had a couple of teeth missing. They continued playing cards and drinking, not looking up. The lawman interrupted. "Good afternoon, men, I hate to disturb you."

"Then don't," one of them said.

"I want you fellows to come with us."

"With y'all," one said. "I ain't got nothing to do with them." He looked at the soldiers.

The one with the long cut on his face said, "We ain't done nothing."

"You have been identified as abductors of some German children and the murder of some Indian parents. We will have someone from the Germans' settlement come identify you."

"We don't know no Germans and who making a big fuss about some stinking Indians. In the army, I got paid to kill 'em." He got up.

Outside, the sheriff pulled his gun to cover the men. Walking past an ally, they were surprised by an armed man. "Hold it! Drop the gun."

The sheriff turned to point but was shot. A scuffle began.

The man holding the pistol fired into the air. "I said hold it, and hand over those arms."

The sarge and corporal obeyed. Taking them from holsters and dropped them on the ground. The three quickly got to their feet. Then put the soldier's fallen weapons into an animal drinking trough full of water and mounted their horses at a nearby hitching post, then rode off. Chato, the Indian who had talked with his sister earlier, ran into the street to help the soldiers. The sarge helped the sheriff to his feet then turned to the Indian.

"There go the scalp hunters who take your children across the border."

"Me get them," the man said. He mounted a pony nearby and fled after the men. Outside town, he rode to a camp where warriors waited. After explaining what happened, they mounted ponies and hurried off.

That night, the bandits made camp. There was no moon. The Indians who knew what the men had done to their people surprised. Then tied and systematically scalped them, tied, with their heads bleeding. They were laid next to a red ant hill. They disturbed the ants to an angry frenzy. The ants had a bloody feast. Days later, an old desert miner rode into town with a donkey pulling a travois with four badly decomposed bodies. Flies buzzed around it. He stopped in the front of the sheriff's office. Curious townspeople who followed also stopped. The sheriff came from his office, examined the corpses, and said, "These are the men who kill Apaches for their scalps. They capture our kids and sell them as sex slaves."

The townspeople talked among themselves then slowly dispersed.

CHAPTER 5

The sarge rode into the tent city where Barbara and the Germans lived. He saw a few boys excitedly watching a fight. Getting close to investigate, he saw Barbara's son, Jim, in the middle of a group, fighting a white boy about his age and size. He observed a moment, saw it was pretty even but decided to break it up before one of them got hurt.

"What's this about, Jim?" he asked.

He said, "I ain't no American. I told him I was and he was a foreigner. He said he was going to be American like the people in town because he is white. I said I was as American as the people in town. The only real Americans are trying to kill us 'cause we settle on their land."

Craves put his arm around him they began to walk. "Boy, you gonna be a fine man. A lot of grown-ups don't understand what you just said. With that head, you got to keep learning. You gonna be able to tell a lot of people things."

They stopped in front of the family's tent. He hollered, "Hello! It's us men. Everybody, descent."

The oldest girl, Shirley, opened the flap that served as a doorway. "Oh, sarge, come in."

He walked into the large tent. The boy stayed outside, "It's too crowded with females. See y'all."

Shirley extended hers, and shook his hand. "Mom's not here but should be soon. Have a seat."

He sat on a small couch in the middle of the tent that had been sectioned off by hanging blankets to make small private spaces. She excused herself and returned to her little sister. "I'm teaching her math and spelling. Mom teaches things she knows later. Jim rides with the boys all the time. The other day they came back from the hills all sweating and said they had been chased by Indians. I was scared almost to death. I asked if they were painted and close to the settlement. They started laughing, falling on the ground, acting foolish. I knew then they were lying."

A horse-drawn carriage arrived in the front. "I believe that's her."

Barbara came inside. Her little girl, Annie-May, rushed to hug her. Shirley did the same.

"Well, what a surprise."

Craves stood and shook her hand. "I told you I was coming to see all of you and find out how you doing. You were busy, but me and the boys enjoyed that fine supper you served the other day. I think everybody who come to the restaurant did," he said.

"Well, Mrs. Sue, the owner, told me to cook my own style. Since then, I've been cooking about half the meals. She was so happy she gave me a raise."

"That's good," he said then thought a moment. "If you ain't tired, lets take a buggy ride."

"It's still dangerous around here. If we're not going too far, I'll be glad to go. I ain't got no buggy. We'll take my little wagon. First, let me freshen a bit."

She went behind one of the blankets hung for privacy. "We have to bring water a ways and do the best we can. All that sand blowing is a mess." Water splashed for a moment.

Shirley asked, "How's Joe doing?"

"He's busy like the rest of us."

"Is he married?"

The sarge thought, *Seems one of the men is on someone's mind.*

"No, he ain't."

In about twenty minutes, Barbara came from behind the partition, clothing changed. Getting close, he smelled the scent of store-brought soap.

"I'm ready," she said.

"Wow, look at you," he replied.

She spun around and watched his gaze.

"Yes, ma'am," he said. "You sho' is some'em."

She took his arm and looked at her daughter. "We'll be back at sundown. Go on and eat. Don't wait for us."

"Have fun, y'all," Shirley said.

One afternoon, Barbara served customers in the restaurant. All the tables were full except one in a corner. Craves, Joe, and Corporal Abraham entered and sat, removing their hats at a table. Close by four people looking at them, seemed annoyed, got up without finishing their meal, then left.

"Barbara, what happened?"

She put her hands on her hips and frowned. "Cussed folk, some of them look at me when I serve and frown. I don't pay them no mind. Mrs. Sue told me I was more important to the place than them."

At that moment, the owner looked from the back and waved. "We only have the special left." The sarge beckoned her to lean closer. "Everything you make is special." Everyone laughed. "It's going to be special for everybody."

They ate, finished, then stood. He asked, "How long before you leave?"

"I got two more hours," she said.

Later, they were drinking beer in the saloon where they hung out. The place was half full. The black gambler sat solo with a deck of cards. Soldiers and civilians sat drinking with black, Indian, and Mexican women.

Craves rose from a table. "I'll see y'all later."

He waited at a stable. Barbara arrived. They shook hands and went inside and got in her wagon.

"I still got this but soon you gonna see an improvement. I'll pay," he said then gave a few coin to the stableman, who smiled and gladly accepted them. They rode off down the street then turned onto a road.

Craves said, "I'm enjoying your company."

"It's only been a few months since John died, but I'm enjoying yours too," she said.

"We know it's been a short time, but I'd like to ask you something."

"Sure, you mean, can you court me?"

He looked surprised. "A woman can see in a man's eyes what's in his head and his heart. He starts getting frisky," she smiled.

Then continued, "Mr. Sarge, I'm about five years your senior and have a house full of children. If you don't think that's too much for you, I'm honored. And yes, Mr. Craves, you call on me, I'll be waiting."

A week passed. One Sunday, Barbara's family, Craves, and Corporal Joe had a picnic. Her son and the German boy—the one he had fought—raced their horses short distances. Barbara hollered, "Don't go far! It's dangerous."

Joe and Shirley held hands and walked a little ways off. "I see Ms. Hazel with some of the ladies or gals as the locals call them."

They stopped by and got orders to go. Barbara said.

"I guess where they work and with people knowing what they do, they expect hostile looks and whispers from customers. They hold their heads high and strut off, minding their business." She continued, "It's not my place to judge anyone, but the thought runs through a woman's mind. Who gets involved with a man who hangs around drinking and gambling in those places? We know them women are known to pass stuff around nobody want."

He knew she meant "the drip" and, in extreme cases, syphilis. Everybody knew the consequences. To put her mind at ease, he said, "Since they work where government army personal frequent, they all agreed to have their"—he bent over and whispered—"money makers checked a few times a month."

He leaned up, laughing. "They don't want to be forced out of business."

She laughed, hugged him then clapped her hands, and continued to laugh louder. "I done heard everything. It's good our soldiers get government-inspected stuff." She continued shaking her head. "Mmmmm mum ain't that something. Government-inspected crotch."

Joe and Shirley walked close, holding hands. Craves came over and whispered, "Remember, she's young." He patted his arm and walked away. Before he got far, Joe grabbed his arm and whispered in his ear, "Ain't her mother a little old for you?"

CHAPTER 6

A large patrol of twenty-five black soldiers lead by a white captain saddled their horses. They were to meet a stage at Rimrock. Rimrock was a dangerous place. Doubtful Cannon was not far from it. Many travelers had been ambushed by Apaches. Outlaws were known to hold up stages. There the captain addressed them. "You men have to be especially vigilant. The patrol that went to round up settlers has not returned. They rode off and soon arrived, where they were overcome with nausea."

"It's the patrol," Craves said.

They put handkerchiefs over their noses. Then were alerted by the sound of an approaching figure. It was the patrol's scout. He had escaped the massacre. The lieutenant decided it would take too long to bury them. He picked three men from the group and told them to return to the fort with the scout. The major would know what to do. He'd probably send wagons to recover the bodies.

A stage coach hurried down a lonely open road. Blue skies reached to the horizons. Dust stirred by the coach and horse's hooves blew into the windows on the restless passengers. The squeak and drumming horse's hooves had happened so long the people, when not dozing, did whatever they could to maintain high spirits. The driver and shotgun guard had seen the same places many times; it was their route. From time to time, they looked to the sides, ready and alert for danger, not to be surprised.

"I sure hope those soldiers show. We done passed Rimrock." He hunched his shoulders. "Where they at? We couldn't just wait. The horses were rested. That's all we could do. We making time the company's glad—that's all."

Two man and a woman traveled inside. "We should be in Tombstone soon," the man said.

"I can't wait to get to work to see those happy faces when the curtain rises," the woman said, "and do my new performance."

One of the men, her agent, said, "The place is booked up. The sponsors are happy you got spirit."

"That's right. Get there, give the crowd their show, then we leave."

The other man, a drummer, traveled the countryside selling women's undergarments. He took a bottle from the inside of his coat, put a little powder from it, on a finger, lifted it to his nose and sniffed. He extended the bottle to the couple. They refused.

The woman said, "I use that when I perform."

"Sometimes," the agent said, "I use it when I'm nervous. And I need something to calm myself. Look." He pointed. The others looked in the direction he pointed. They saw a large group of Indians on a faraway ridge.

"Oh my god," the woman said.

The drummer hollered, "Hey, up there! Are those savages friendly?"

The guard hollered, "If they were, they wouldn't be that many! We ain't sticking around to find out."

He hollered, "Hold on inside!" and began whipping the horses. The horses, already galloping, sped up. The Indians had been walking their horses, jumped on them, and galloped from the ridge. The stage was moving at top speed. The Indians reached the road. Their ponies picked up speed. They began hollering. The guard put the shotgun down, grabbed a Winchester, chambered it, aimed, and began shooting. The Indians, getting close, using rifles, returned fire. After a hasty ride each side, firing on the other, a bugle could be heard in the distance.

The driver said, "That's them colored soldiers boys stationed at the fort."

The bugle continued blowing and got louder; the men approached. The Indians in range of the coach heard the sound and began slowing. After seeing the number of men approaching, they turned and galloped toward the hills. The soldiers passed the coach firing in hot pursuit. Some Indians fell from their horses. Others fled onward.

The agent said, "Now I need some nerve calmers." He reached into a breast pocket, pulled a bottle from it, and guzzled away. The soldiers returned. The passengers were out of the stage. They cheered.

"Happy to see you, men." The drummer patted his bald head. "I don't have nothing here." He ran his finger across his throat. "I like this the way it is."

The woman said, "I'm Helen McCurry. Wherever I'm entertaining, you men are welcome free. Down in Tombstone, the drinks are on me."

The stage driver said, "I have a mail pouch. I'll give it to you when we get to town."

CHAPTER 7

There was a large ceremony at the fort. Civilians were on hand to watch. The soldiers were black with white officers. Barbara Ann's family, including the oldest, Shirley, was present. The soldiers were lined, dressed in their finest uniforms, and for the special occasion, dress medal helmets. Each stepped forward when his name was called to receive a medal.

When Sergeant Craves stepped forward, his was presented by the major who also added, You are also on this occasion being promoted to sergeant first class of the Tenth United States Cavalry." He handed patches to the sergeant. "Please have these sewn on."

After the awards had been presented, the civilians stood and mingled with the men, congratulating and hugging them. Some of the town's saloon women were among the civilians. Corporal Joe looked at Shirley, who stood a moment then ran to hug him. Looking over her shoulder to see her family, seeing them busy with other men, she quickly kissed his lips.

Inside the fort's office, the company Lieutenant McCurry came from another office. He told Corporal Abraham, who was standing at attention, "The major will see you now." Abraham entered the major's office, snapped to attention, and saluted.

The major, sitting behind a desk, returned the salute then began. "This is out of the ordinary, soldier, you wanted to skip the chain of command. I hope this is an emergency. I only accepted your request because you were among the men honored today."

The corporal began to stutter, "Sir . . . I . . . just got a letter, sir . . . from Ala . . . bama . . . sir." He continued to stutter more until he finished. "Before I got stationed here, I was in Georgia doing reconstructioning down there. I had a whole lot of run-ins with them local folk. I mean, the white people, sir."

"Yes, yes, go on," the major, in a hurry, said.

He continued, "I was always afraid when the federal troops left. The whites would take advantage of the unprotected colored folk. I want to take some leave time maybe up to three months to see how I can protect my kin. Then I will return."

"Your job is to protect the frontier."

He insisted. "Sir . . . then just for a month. He finished.

The major trumpeted. "That will be all, corporal."

Abraham saluted and did an about-face. As he was leaving, the major said, "Other organizations will protect your people."

CHAPTER 8

A new buggy traveled on a dusty road.

Sergeant Craves with Barbara arrived outside a small building still under construction. Darkness had just fallen. The twinkle of little stars could be seen.

Craves said, "This is the surprise. It's not far from the fort. Me being a noncommissioned officer, I can move outside the fort closer to town. I figured since I'm going to have a big family."

She smiled. He returned it.

"Yes, that means I'm fumbling around, trying to ask you to marry me. Hmm, I guess I just did." He looked at her smiling face as he fumbled in his pocket. He took a ring from it, lifted her hand, and slipped the ring on a finger. "Now will you marry me?"

She answered with teary eyes. "Oh yes, Sarge, oh yes." They kissed then hugged.

"Come on in. There is only a roof on one of the rooms."

"I hope it don't rain."

They walked into the room that would become the bedroom. It had a double bed but no fixtures. He lit two candles that were stuck in empty beer bottles. One he put on the floor, the other he left on the table.

"How cozy," she said. They hugged, kissed, and laid on the bed, rolling around for a few minutes. Finally, he sat, yanked off his shirt, sat on the bed, and yanked his boots off. He stood again. She was now standing.

She said, "I don't want to mess this up," then removed the dress from her shoulders and let it fall with her slip inside. Slipping out of them, she moved toward her man with only bloomers. He kissed one breast then the other. She sat on the bed, removed her underpants, then curled up. In one swift movement, the sarge leaned and blew the candle on the table out then the one on the floor. The room was now in darkness. The silence was broken, "Oh, honey. Yes, yes, yes. Oh my, Sarge. I love you."

Hours later, the sarge shook her. "Honey, it's morning."

She awake. "What time is it?"

Stars showed through the uncovered next room.

"Wait a minute." He reached into his pants on the small table and pulled out a pocket watch. "It's getting about five. You said you were going back to your kids last night."

Laughing teasingly, she said, "It was your fault, all that carrying on. Turned out being both our fault. It's earlier but getting late, I have to go to work. Where's the water?"

"There's not much, only a couple of buckets," he said.

"They will do," she said. "One for me, one for you."

"No, womenfolk need more than us men. I'll wait until I get to the barracks. Remember, soldiers camp out in the dirt."

At the fort, Craves jumped from the buggy. "Thanks for dropping me off."

She leaned and gave him a kiss on the lips. "I enjoyed myself."

"Me too," he said.

She leaned and kissed him again thats for many nights in the future. He mumbled, "Sure, 'nuff." The buggy drove off.

CHAPTER 9

Craves walked into the bunkhouse barracks. The men were in serious forms of grooming, some shaved; others bathed.

The corporal approached. "Musta been good." He kiddingly patted the sarge's shoulder.

A soldier on a corner bunk said, "No disrespect, sarge. I see the way that dress moves when she walks, whatever, moving it gotta be good."

"If y'all don't want my boot up yours, forget how her dress moves. What's in it is all mine. Y'all wondering. Yeah, we had a good time, it's gonna last to we getting married."

"You said you was gonna do it, Pop," Joe said. "Y'all hear that? He gonna be my father-in law."

The men together said, "Congratulations, Sarge, and congratulations, Corporal Joe."

Craves looked at the corporal. "What's going on?"

"You heard right," Joe answered. "Me and Shirley are gonna get married. I asked her last night. Her mom wasn't around, I asked anyway."

Craves said, "She's only a child."

Joe said, "Only in age. She's almost sixteen."

"What's Barbara gonna say?"

"I thinks she likes me. I mean, in a family way. If she hadn't thought about it, I'm sure she will come around and accept me. I mean, me and her daughter you know."

Kiddingly, Craves said, "Ah, I don't know if I want you in my family."

From a few bunks, Cherokee said with his bad accent, "Y'all stay in the same family. Too bad she ain't got more big daughters. Tell her write and tell some of her female family that they got a bunch of lonely colored soldiers over here."

Abrams, Willis, and a few others hollered in unison. "Speak for yourself, Cherokee. We like the Fillies over at the saloon. All they want is us to spend money. All we want is some honey. No headaches."

Barbara arrived home. Her children ran to welcome her. She held her hand in front of Shirley. "Look."

She responded, "Oh mom."

Annie May, the little one close, asked, "What's that mom?"

Jim put his hands on his hip. "You don't know nothing. That means the sarge is gonna be our new daddy. Right, mom?"

"Sure," she said.

Shirley said, "I got something to tell you, mom."

"I'm listening."

The children gathered to listen.

"I'm getting married too. Joe didn't have a ring but said he would get one."

"Gal, what you talking about?"

"He asked me last night."

"But, child, you are so young."

"I was worried and wondered what you would say."

"Soldiers' lives are dangerous. I'm gonna marry one. I guess it's all right for you."

Jim jumped around. "There are gonna be men around besides me!"

Barbara closed her eyes and leaned. "You just lost your pappy. This is a lot for a fifteen-year-old."

She said, "I'm almost sixteen. How old were you when you and dad married?"

Her mother breathed then quietly said fifteen.

CHAPTER 10

A large group assembled at the base chapel. The two women each holding a bouquet of flowers stood, ready to enter the holy bounds of matrimony.

"This is a good idea, mom. We're both gonna be newlyweds."

They were joined by the elegantly dressed men in formal uniforms. They took the women's arms. The piano played "Here Comes the Bride." The couples slowly began their last walk as singles. They arrived at the podium. The ceremony was given by a black army chaplain. Without interruptions, they were pronounced man and wife at the same time. The assemblage was happy. Saloon women there wept. The beautiful woman, Hazel Craves's friend, quietly looked on. The couples rushed down the aisles. Outside they were covered with confetti.

Soldiers and civilians gathered around a punch bowl in a corner. Cherokee and a bunch of soldiers poured liquor from a small bottle into their cups. The Indian scout who always accompanied them stood with his woman. When the bottle came in front of him, he extended his to receive a share. The woman, standing near, put her hand in front of the bottle. The soldier offering it looked at her. She poked her mouth out and made a face, shaking her head. He continued to the next extended cup. Both

Tecumseh and Cherokee were accompanied by doves. Tecumseh's date, Daisy, was a dark, unmixed colored woman. Cherokee had hooked up with Happyness. Chato's sister, Daisy, had begun teaching him better English. Cherokee, on the other hand, spoke broken English along with his native tongue. Happyness spoke little English.

A piano, fiddle, and banjo played music. Couples danced. Soldiers, with saloon women. Barbara and Craves finished dancing and were joined on the floor by Mrs. Sue and her husband, the restaurant owners. They hugged Barbara then left the ballroom. Barbara and Craves walked to their table. A large cake was cut; portions were placed on small plates. A group gather to be served. Hazel spoke, "I've seen you at the restaurant, Mrs. Craves. You are a lucky woman. I'm happy you snagged a man all the girls including me thought was unsnaggable. Again, congratulations."

Craves stood by. She held her arms out hugged Barbara then asked, "Any objection to me hugging your husband?"

Barbara looked on, puzzled, stuttered, "Oh . . . no—go ahead."

Hazel hugged Craves and said, "Good luck to you both."

"Thanks," Barbara said. "You are so thoughtful, but from now on, the sergeant is going to get all the hugs he needs at home. I don't mind him having a few beers with his buddies—a few, mind you—but no hugs."

"I understand," Hazel said.

People standing by clapped.

Cherokee told the man with the bottle, "A little more please, you know the special stuff." Tecumseh held out his cup too. After receiving and downing them, they, and their dates, danced around with the music.

CHAPTER 11

Months later, Craves and Joe rode going to the house they shared with their brides.

Craves said, "The kid getting it that way after all these years. He wasn't as old as you."

"What, all those men he killed?" Craves continued. "The William Bonney I knew first worked as a regulator, a private detective like the Pinkertons. His boss was murdered by competition. That started the Lincoln County War, more like a fraud. Both sides hired known gunmen who didn't hesitate to kill. There was no turning back. The kid revenged the killing of his boss. When people tried stopping him, they wound up dead. I think I told you how he got pinned up in a burning house they fired into. It fell apart. That lucky son of a gun got away. We rode up. A Chinese woman and a couple of his buddies gave up to save their lives. The Possy, trying to kill Billy, didn't care about them. Seems he always escaped, with death riding his back. The state governor offered him a pardon. He went on killing. They said it was twenty-one men he killed. He went down by the border to see his senorita. His old buddy turned sheriff showed up and killed him for a big reward on his head then collected it."

Barbara sat in the bedroom in the finished house. Craves walked in.

"Well, two of those men who got mail from back south took off. They had told everybody and tried to get leave and couldn't. Everybody was mad about things changing down there. We knew them old masters and poor white class was gonna accept us as equals anyway. I ain't got mail from my folk. Nobody I know can write, and I couldn't read nothing they sent anyway."

She said, "I can feel and understand what they are up against. I don't care about them accepting me. I just wanna be left alone. Back in Kansas, I've seen some good and a lot of bad whites. The good tried to help us. People like John Brown was called fanatics. The bad were so bad, what extreme things the good did, the bad did ten times worse. They had all kinds of riders and raiders. Bloody Bill Anderson and his cutthroats. Quantrill, the Missouri Red Legs. All of them burned wherever they had a chance. Who was gonna stop them? We just wanted to be free to work and run our lives the way we saw fit. That was so hard for them to understand. We sure were thankful when the government came down, and shot, and blew up the place. Thing done changed a lot, some things still the same." She looked serious then smiled. "When you start writing, somebody's gonna read what you wrote. When they learn to write, you will be able to read their letters."

He said, "You know I'm trying. How that thing go? Little boy blue, come blow your horn, the sheep in the corn—"

She stopped him. "No, the sheep's in the meadow."

He remembered. "Yeah. The sheep's in the meadow, the cow's in the corn."

She put a pencil in his hand and a notebook in front of them. He took her hand and pulled her to him. She protested, half laughing and giggling. "No, we have work to do."

"I guess I'm just thickheaded in some ways," he said. He put her on his lap and covered her with kisses. She fumbled playfully, giggling. "Stop. Stop."

He said, "That stuff is for later. I got other homework in mind. I'm glad God took that rib and made y'all."

"You gonna hurt the baby, stop." She giggled.

CHAPTER 12

The two very pregnant women walked from the general store. Their husbands carried bags then loaded a wagon. The buggy carriage they used was too small to accommodate four people with supplies. Leaving town, they passed the soldiers' saloon hangout. A woman standing outside saw them and hurried through the batwing door. A few women hurried outside and waved. Hazel was one. She hollered, "I see y'all been taking care of them men."

Barbara patted her stomach then her daughter's. "Whatever they want and need, they get." She smiled.

Barbara and Shirley cleaned the house. Shirley said, "Joe been telling me soon there ain't gonna be no more buffalo or antelope. And the Indians on the Plains are gonna starve. He said it happened to the Indians who depended on beaver, but at least they could fish. He said the beavers were killed for their skins so people back East and overseas could make hats out of them. The same thing's happening now. Those people making buffalo coats and stuff. He said he told me that so I would know what's happening around us. He said he won't be happy until he gets some college knowledge. You see, Mom, he's a dreamer. Nothing big like people making steel or building railroads, but he said we gotta be smart 'cause people coming from all over the world to fill their dreams and we go to compete."

"Sure sounds big. I hope he doesn't get disappointed. I hope you don't either." Barbara said.

While both were expecting, they thought it would be wonderful if they were to deliver at the same time or on the same day.

Barbara said, "I told Craves about our wish. All he said was 'that would be something.' Sometimes I forget he doesn't know about nothing but soldiering." She smiled. "Still I have grown to love him. I went to the doctor in town about some cramp medicine. I didn't say anything about the baby. You know he stuttered, 'Lady, da-lady, I can't deliver your baby.' I thought, a doctor who can't deliver a baby. My baby. Then I thought, he's half drunk all the time. Maybe it's better and for the good. I remembered Mrs. Grossman. I can hardly understand her when she talks, but she said that in her country, she had been a midwife and delivered lots of healthy babies. I'm thinking about her helping me and you too."

Shirley said, "I'm still hoping they are simultaneously born. That would be something. Mine's gonna be your baby's niece or nephew."

The sarge sat rubbing his hands. He had never been a father. Mrs. Grossman came out of the adjoining room wearing a broad smile. He didn't understand her accent but knew her smile meant everything was all right. He hurried into the next room. The baby was wrapped in a clean sheet. He hurried to his still-sweating woman holding the crying baby.

She said, "Baby, that was tough." She let out a sigh. "Real tough."

Shirley waddled into the room, her belly extended. Joe followed. "Congratulations, mom. I'd love to hug you, but see, I can't bend."

Joe asked, "Sarge, you still got some of that corn stuff your people sent?"

Craves, standing by his wife, said, "I thought you don't drink."

"I thought I'd start," he said.

"Barbara hid it. I found out where. Come on."

The two men toasted each other.

"Here's to you, Pops," Joe said. He was not a drinking man, and the whiskey soon showed it affect his words began to slur.

Craves returned the toast. "Here's to you, son."

After an hour of the same, a baby's cry was heard.

Joe asked, "What time is it?"

Craves reached into his pocket, took out his watch, and looked.

"It's twenty minutes after twelve. They ain't simultaneous but close. Thanks, God. Thanks, Shirley."

They toasted again. Mrs. Grossman came out of the room. "It's a girl."

The men glad it was born healthy didn't care about its sex. Now full of drinks, both rose from theirs chairs and stumbled into the adjoining room.

CHAPTER 13

Mrs. Sue, the owner of the restaurant where Barbara worked, had invited her and her family to her church to meet the congregation. The sarge, her daughter, and Joe accompanied her. The children were left in the settlement with Mrs. Grossman's family because she did not know how they would be received. They all had casual relations in town with shopkeepers, the sheriff, and others. Normally, the soldiers attended service with the black chaplain at the fort. The African American community was small. The soldiers' presence had become as common as others. They came and went like everyone. Other blacks passed through town on their way to silver mines close to Tombstone to work. Soiled doves—white, black, Mexican, and Indian—slept early on Sundays. Weekends were their busiest days and nights. They all were exhausted and had little desires for anything. Mrs. Sue's family arrived the same time Barbara's did. Both parties left their carriages and wagons close to church where other members had theirs. After welcoming one another, they entered. Service had begun. The place was three quarters full. The preacher, reading scripture, stopped and looked up. Mrs. Sue had informed him of her planned arrival with the guests. When she first approached Barbara with the proposal to join her family, Barbara hesitated until she was assured the preacher was in agreement with their coming because it was open to the community. When they entered, the whole congregation turned. Some gasped and whispered to one another. Some pointed.

One stood, made a face, and shouted, "I ain't going to worship with them!" He pulled and pushed his family to the entrance; another family followed. They stomped from the building. It was Jeb the Reb and one of his friends and family.

The preacher said, "Folks, this is the Lord's house. If we all are going to the same glory, we'll be there together. The one's going to the other place. I'm sure will find their kind. Let's sing."

They began, "Let's gather at the river, / the beautiful, beautiful river, / the wonderful place of God."

CHAPTER 14

Two years later, Joe received a scholarship to a Christian college in Ohio. It, like other of its kind, had been around since pre–Civil War days. All had actively engaged in the abolitionist movement and underground railroad. One of the most famous was Wilberforce College, named after the Englishman William Wilberforce, who aggressively argued and lectured against the Atlantic slave trade because of its extreme cruelty. Eventually, he lectured the British parliament in the late 1700s and got it abolished. When Joe's family arrived and settled, he began studying but joined the army reserves, where his experiences on the frontier earned him promotions. Now Sergeant Joseph Washington added to his income a salary from teaching at a military school that prepared boys to be soldiers—a low-paying but respected profession. Shirley took care of her daughter named Brenda and maintained the house and continued developing the trade she and her mother worked when they both had young babies to care for. Barbara quit her job in town. They made dresses, tablecloths, drapes, and other articles that were sold to neighbors and people in town.

In Ohio, with both their earnings, she was soon able to buy one of the new marvels—a sewing machine. With it, she developed into a seamstress. She became pregnant again when not busy, she kept in contact with her mother and adopted father by writing letters. Her mother read the letters despite slow-learning Craves. The nearby town was growing like many in the industrial age. Immigrants arrived and lived under crowded conditions; it was the first time many had money. The little they made was more than they were ever going to have in their countries of origin. Competition between each group was great. Mills belched smoke and soot that gave the sky a cloudy look and funny smell. Horse-drawn streetcars added to congested streets. Joe and Shirley were accustoming themselves like the immigrants and were also prospering.

CHAPTER 15

Sergeant Craves and a troop of twenty men had been patrolling the surrounding countryside. Hostiles were still active. There had been few homesteads raided because the settlers had moved close to town. With a twenty-man patrol on their trail, the hostiles kept on the move. They lived on the meager food they hunted or on what people left behind. They roamed in bands of fifteen to twenty-five. Being small, they had mobility and had sworn to fight to the death. Twenty or so well-armed soldiers would represent an invitation to an early death why hurried it.

The soldiers returned to the fort; an alert had gone out. They were informed kidnappers had struck again. This time, they entered the German school at the settlement and abducted children who had been studying. They were taken with their teacher who had been coming from town to hold special classes for the youngsters. Craves, upon hearing about it, hollered, "No, oh, no, no, no. The poor things."

He left the patrol and rode off. The teacher had come to the settlement for a small group of children. The Reb's daughter accompanied her to return later to town. Craves entered the house of stillness. Barbara was pregnant again; she had three months left before delivery. A strange illness had overcome her. She was told to rest a lot. There had been no final diagnosis. She began running a fever. Her son, Jim, now eleven, lay close. He had been shot. Her daughter stood holding her hand. The house was filled with Germans from the settlement. Mrs. Grossman was there. One of Jim's friends explained, "We saw a bunch of men coming out of the school. They had the teacher and students. All of them were tussling and screaming. A man knocked the teacher out and threw her on a horse. Each of the children were put in front of one of the men on their horses. There were about seven or eight of them. They saw us running toward them and began shooting. We ducked Jim got shot in the shoulder. Hansel was wounded in the leg. His head got grazed by a bullet. After they rode off, we ran to the fields for the men. They came in a hurry. Some had rifles ready for attacks from Indians. The men didn't have horses and couldn't follow them."

Craves hollered, "They took Annie May! Barbara, they got poor Annie."

In town, Jeb the Reb cried tears in front of a bunch of men. "My Suzanna! I said I don't care how many of y'all go. I'm going. I told that dame teacher to bring my daughter straight home. Now she done got kidnapped with a bunch of foreigners and probably the little black thing she likes to hang with. Like I said, I don't care how many y'all going. I'm going."

The commander at the Fort Colonel Simpson decided to send a seasoned captain to rescue the teacher and children. "Men, I wish you luck. I sent a telegram ahead to Sonora, Mexico, telling them to be on the lookout for kidnappers who might cross into their territory."

The town posse were all volunteers. The sheriff remained and continued his duties. The colonel knew of Jeb's hostility toward blacks and was not in a position to control the posse that was organized. The black troops were under the command of an officer and Sergeant Jenkins Craves. He knew the sergeant as being bright and levelheaded but, because of personal interest, did not feel comfortable. The Indian scout was put in command of scouting. The two half Indians, Tecumseh and Cherokee, were part of the platoon. The group included four towns people and Jeb. Before they left the Fort, the captain explained, "That bunch we going after got a half-day start. We don't know how good they know the country. One thing's sure, they are headed for the border.

Jeb said, "I can track as good as them Indians. I used to scout for the Grey Ghost, remember?"

The sarge told him, "This is an army patrol. You'll take orders from us."

He responded, "I ain't takin' orders from you. I'm taking them from the captain."

They rode off. Jeb mumbled to one of the townspeople, "If it wasn't for that captain, no way I'd trust myself along with them. They got us outnumbered."

One of the townsmen said, "I don't know whose side you're on. I'm with the patrol."

The captain said, "Men, we gallop to make time, then walk the horses to give them and us a rest. We don't wanna wear neither out. Tonight, there will be a full moon. We will take advantage of it— trot through the night and walk tomorrow when the sun gets hot."

They rode through the night. He said, "Old Moses's place is ahead. It's a trading post. He gives the best deals. Without him,

Indians would be out of things they need even considering that, he didn't gamble, he sent his kids and grandchildren to stay with relatives."

When they arrived, the place looked run-down and shabby. Nobody seemed to be around. The men dismounted and started toward the well to get water for themselves and the animals. While they were walking, they saw a bad omen a dead dog laid to the side. They rushed to the well. The dead body of Moses floated on top of the water. Some rushed to the house. Inside, they found Moses's elderly wife's raped, mutilated, defiled body.

The sarge said, "It was them, Indian didn't do this."

The captain said, "No race would claim that. They are animals. How long ago, you guess?"

"It happened this morning," Craves said.

The captain said, "We don't have much time. The border is not far. Make a shallow grave that won't take time. They know they are being followed but don't know we cut the distance."

Jeb spoke up, "Ain't no border gonna stop me."

The captain said, "You don't have a uniform on. I can't stop you. I'm sure the sergeant shares your feeling. If we don't reach them before they cross, I will attempt to stop men under my command from an illegal crossing, but you go on your own."

They traveled on and found one of the men dead, his elbow swollen with venom from a rattlesnake bite. Jeb said, "Good. I wish all, but the children are gobbled up by a whole pit of snakes and left to feed the varmint."

They quickened their pace then found the teacher laid out on a blanket, bloodied. She had been savagely raped and was near death. The men dismounted.

The captain said, "We are too close to stop. They did this for savageness but also knew we would slow to help this helpless wretch. Sergeant, do what's necessary. We will continue."

Craves said, "I need men," Tecumseh, Cherokee and a townsman who knew the women volunteered to stay. Craves said, "A wagon was at the trading post."

"Go get it. We will be back tomorrow. Let her rest and recuperate a little."

He jumped on his horse, spurred it, then galloped to catch the patrol. He arrived at a hilltop where the others had stopped to observe the kidnappers riding onshore trying to find a shallow place across the Rio Grande. Some places, they knew were too deep. The seven children were still with them. The soldiers were hesitant to shoot, fearing the children might get hit.

The men saw the soldiers had arrived and were observing them, hesitating because each had a child sitting in front of him on horseback. They entered the rushing water. The soldiers dashed after them. Each turned with pistols and blasted, hoping to frighten their pursuers. Some horses reared, dumping the children, the men hardened to frontier life held on to the horses' saddles, bridles, or tails, and splashed for dear life. They were halfway across when firing came from the opposite side. Mexican soldiers had appeared and were using rifles to carefully shoot the outlaws from their saddles. Several troops entered the water. Craves hurried to join them. A few kidnappers began swimming their horses down river. A running battle ensured until the escaping men dead floated on the water. Soldiers swam to rescue the children. Jeb's horse, frightened, reared and threw him. He screamed. The onlookers couldn't imagine. He began thrashing and splashing around in a panic. "I can't swim!" He went underwater, rose, and spat water. "I can't swim! Help!"—*splash splash*—"Help me!"

Going down, a black soldier swimming close dove and pulled him to the top. They reached the shore. Jeb's arms were wrapped around the black man. His eyes rolled in his head. The rescue party checked the children. All shook with fright but smiled. Suzanna, Annie May, and the German kids were all right. The two men's daughters ran to them and jumped into their arms. They looked across the rushing river. The Mexican soldiers, ready to leave, waved. They waved back, then left, riding in different directions. One of the black soldiers told another, "I thought all them crackers could swim."

Reaching the fort, they found the surrounding area quiet. German measles had overwhelmed the settlement. It had been quarantined. The strange illness that plagued Barbara was diagnosed as diphtheria. Mrs. Grossman used remedies from the old country. The measles, a communicable disease, ran its course. Craves, not allowed in the sealed-off community, stayed at the fort's barracks. After a week, Jim came and stood in front of the fort gate. A guard came out and said, "Son, you are from a quarantined community."

Jim began crying and slowly said, "I just wanted to tell my father, the sarge, that Momma died." He turned and ran.

In a few days, Craves with the two scouts from Oklahoma returned to the settlement. The two women the scouts had dated and settled with came forward. Daisy, who spoke English, said, "The quarantine is over."

"We know." The scouts hugged their women.

Craves went into the house. Mrs. Grossman was there. She held her hands in front of her, made a cross, then said sorry. "Mr. Craves, your missus was told by the doctor the baby could possibly make it. She, because of the multiple diseases she had fought, probably would not. Left with a choice, she said, 'Save the baby. Tell the sarge I love him.' Craves put his head in his hands and sobbed.

CHAPTER 16

Joe Jr., Shirley, her brother, and sisters stood at the train station with Craves. It was a solemn occasion.

"I will be mother to all of them. Thanks, Father, again for seeing Mother's funeral was taken care of. We will never forget you. You will always be loved by us all."

The conductor hollered, "All aboard!"

The train let off steam with a loud sound. The party began moving. Joe and Craves hugged. Shirley on the side hurried and did the same. He leaned and hugged the children: Joe, the kids, and Shirley with the baby in an arm boarded the train then left.

With his wife dead and the children gone, Craves spent the next couple of years doing regular duties—the off hours he spent with men, playing cards at the saloon and drowning his sorrow. The doves, knowing his grief and out of respect for his deceased, they had known cheered him without getting close.

Tecumseh and Cherokee, with their women, had built houses close. Tecumseh married Daisy. Soon a baby was born.

Tecumseh, Daisy, and her two children—one by her new husband—went to East Texas to meet her family. She had four younger brothers and three sisters, some younger, some older. They all lived in a small farming community. Some were married. Others lived in open unions. All went to the Colored Community Baptist Church. The family immediately liked her husband with his coal-black wavy hair. The colored in those days thought anything that showed a person wasn't full-blood Negro had desirable traits. It wasn't unusual to see a half Indian. Indians were to the North a ways, in any local many blacks had mixed blood. Daisy's sister, Ruby, had two light-skinned children, probably fathered by one of the light-skinned men who lived there. Her other sister, Pearl's, were very light and probably fathered by a white man. When Daisy talked of her experiences (she embellished), everyone was fascinated. Going West and working as a washerwoman was more adventurous than working in the fields or cleaning as a domestic at white women's houses in town. She told them later she had gotten a job at a café where she met her man, got legally married, and started a family; it was quite an accomplishment. All her brothers worked in or around town, plowing fields and planting the cotton harvest. The big moneymaker, cotton, was baled then shipped north from Galveston or on the Mississippi. It all wound up in northern factories making textiles. One of her cousins was an elementary school teacher who invited the couple to visit. Tecumseh wore his uniform. The civilians were amazed. None had ventured West and seldom had seen uniformed men.

The school only had one large room. When Tecumseh was asked to introduce himself, he explained he had been assigned to various frontier forts in Western territories. When younger kids asked questions, they immediately were answered by zealous older students showing how smart they were.

One girl commented, "It must be dangerous out there where Indians kill and scalp people."

He answered, "They fight for their land and survival for their families. Some whites kill and scalp them."

A little boy asked, "Why do they do that, Tecumseh?"

"Because they get money for the scalps, even women's and little children's."

A girl said, "Wow, I'm glad I'm not an Indian."

Tecumseh said, "My father is Indian."

A boy said, "You don't look red."

He answered, "It's inside me."

A girl asked, "Is that the reason you talk funny and have a funny name?"

One hot day, Phillip, one of Daisy's brothers, plowed a field with a single mule. Three black cowboys rode to a stop close by.

They had two unsaddled horses with them. Phillip stopped work and took the straps from his shoulders that were attached to the mule and plow. He walked to where the three men had dismounted. They wore chaps over their pants and introduced themselves as Tom Tatters, James Baker, and Harry Wilson.

"I'm Phill Moor," the working man said.

Tom began, "We've been driving a herd north across Indian country to the railhead in Dodge City, Kansas. We are looking for some men who would like to be wranglers. I don't know how much you make. Our outfit pays thirty a month for sure. Maybe a bonus in Dodge. We're not bosses, mind you, or foremen, but they told us to see if we could round up some hands. It don't matter if you can't ride. A lot of us didn't at first. All we'd known was mules and donkeys. Me and him"—he pointed to one of the others—"was picking cotton. We both heard about this and joined. Now we ride like any cowboy."

"You said thirty a month. That's a lot being it would be mine and not have to share with nobody." Is the food free, "yes" he was told.

A buggy driven by a white man was seen coming. The man, Mr. Magee, arrived. "What y'all boys doing stopping him from working?"

Tom said, "We are from the Double X & Y. We are looking for hands to help run a herd to Kansas."

Mr. Magee said, "The Double X & Y? Why, that's old Dave Fettermen's outfit. He used to be a ranger. Y'all work for him?"

Dave Fettermen was known all over Texas; he had a ranch forty miles away.

"Yes, sir, we're some of his cowhands. We offered your worker thirty dollars a month plus board. It's up to him."

Phill took his hat off. "Pardon, sir, I don't make that kind of money ever. I could help pay money my folk owe you for food at your store."

Mr. Magee said, "Boy, after all that I've done for you. I always treated you good, ain't I?"

Phill stuttered, "Yes, sir, but thirty a month sounds like a prayer answered. I can help my momma and sisters who ain't grown. I'm going."

Tom said, "You gotta ride bareback."

Mr. Magee reached in his buggy and brought out a Winchester. "If y'all come back and try to get more of my help, I'm gonna use this." He waved the rifle. "Now tell Fettermen that." He whipped the horse; the buggy rode off.

Phill said, "I gotta go tell my folk and get some clothes."

Tom said, "We have plenty, even these." He pointed to the chaps he and the others wore.

Phill said, "Some other fellows might want to go, let's get outta here before his boss comes back for his mule and plow. I know he's mad. "Real mad," one said.

CHAPTER 17

Tecumseh took his wife and their children to visit his adopted parents at Fort Sill, Oklahoma, where he and Cherokee had met Craves years earlier. He found out Shedina, in the four years they had been gone, had raised a little boy she named Craves Jr. They called him Little Sarge. When he and this family returned to Arizona to continue his duty, he informed Craves of his unknown growing son back in Oklahoma.

The sarge responded, "The hell you say? That ain't nothing to josh about."

Tecumseh explained, "Sarge, I like you like the older brother I never had—an almost a father. I'd never joke about something like that."

Sergeant Craves, knowing about his growing son, was rejuvenated with renewed spirit and a heightened reasons to be happy. He explained his reason for asking and received a month furlow, and to wire for more if needed.

He arrived at Fort Sill and went to the town close by. Some old friends were still there. Some were married with families; others had remained single. They all continued with their military careers. Some knew about his son; none of them knew of his arrangement with the young woman. He went to visit the old family and was welcomed. They knew their adopted son who visited probably told him about the growing boy. None expected he would want to renew the relation with the boy's mother, but she had grown from a fine girl to a fine-looking woman. She thought he had probably brought a little something to give but mostly wanted to visit his boy. When he explained his still-strong feelings for her and his desire to give his name formally, she was shocked and overjoyed. What luck—many women her age bore one or several for one or several men. Some were the outside woman to a married man; other men planted seeds around with little consideration for a child's future. They married and spent their time at her family home in her small room. The youth of the attractive woman overwhelmed the man whose wife had passed a few years earlier. His heart, with suppressed passion, accelerated again with love and lust.

He enjoyed a long, happy stay and accepted the officer's offer and extended his stay.

He returned to Arizona alone as before; his woman didn't want to travel west.

They kept a correspondence through friends who wrote and read their letters. Months later, when he returned to visit, she explained she was glad he married her but felt the relation shouldn't continue. She never wanted to live a soldier's life, and he liked his career. She knew he hadn't gotten over his love for the wife who had passed. He mumbled her name often in his sleep. She confessed to a prior relation she had when they married with a local who worked in town. They planned to marry when she divorced. She felt it would be better for both of them. He agreed. The marriage had lasted less than a year and was over; he would see his son when he had a chance.

CHAPTER 18

In the passing years, Sergeant Craves was assigned and reassigned to forts and, temporarily, ones in New Mexico and territories recently admitted into the Union. Frontier days were ending. The Native Americans had been overwhelmed. The soldier part of that change was not glorious. They were not passive observers but had help bring it about. They never considered themselves special when they engaged Native Americans just equals. They didn't take advantage of the subdued race but later spent years, being they were colored, as mediators of disputes whenever the government's jurisdiction was involved. Range wars took place in places like Wyoming. Old frontiersmen like Tom Horn, who couldn't adapt, became unfortunate victims. New Mexico, Arizona, and Oklahoma were still territories. The Black units were present when Indian territory was opened to white settlement with the Oklahoma Land Rush. During and before the 1880s through the 1890s, they did duty on Crow, Apache, Sioux, Kickapoo, and other new established reservations. Duties were mostly keeping settlers off them and keeping bootleggers out. Selling liquor to Native Americans at the time was illegal. Many natives grumbled at taking orders from the blacks. Little did they know white people in general during those time though any one not white were subject to subhuman behavior.

They did not consider white soldiers who treated them with disgust and contempt, most being poor and at the bottom of society, felt superior to them. They were a lot better off with colored soldiers.

Craves received a letter from Joe. It explained he didn't want to seem incapable of handling his problems, but he would like the help of his old friend.

Craves had kept in touch over the years with the family and talked on the new invention called a telephone. They seemed prosperous and happy. Curious, knowing his longtime friend wouldn't make an unreasoned request, he bordered a train in Denver to Indian territory. There, he rode a horse through the vast land, stopping to visit old family and friends in one town. He met a tall, gangly black deputy US marshal named Bass Reeves, who patrolled a large area and had gained fame as a lone ranger.

He spoke several Native American languages, used in the area. A coworker that accompanied him at the time was Native American. Reeves was known to give silver dollars to friends and acquaintances. The man, a farmers slave had defiantly beaten his former owner during the Civil War when he was a teen in Texas and ran to Indian territory. Before he retired, he would arrest over three thousand men and kill fourteen. Impressed with the man, Craves though about helping him. After all, they were both agents of the US government. After considering it a day, he let the idea pass. Joe had received a telegram saying he would be there soon, he wanted to spend time with his extended family and the growing teens he had had with Barbara. If he had stayed, who knows what complication may have developed. He bid the man good luck; he'd see him under different circumstances another time.

He continued through the mountains and took a train in Iowa to Chicago. There, he stayed a few days, wearing his uniform all the time. In those days, army personnel wore uniforms often. He was surprised after leaving the West that the further east he went, people stopped pointed, and said, "Look! A colored soldier." He stared at the tallest building he had ever seen and the telephone lines helping build the nation. He and his men had strung many across western states.

While there, he went to a colored neighborhood. Progressive spirit abounded. A variety of businesses catered to the community. Some men worked in the stockyards, steel mills, and industries downtown as porters. The women were domestics in private homes and public buildings. Their spiritual needs were met by small, mostly storefront churches.

Everything added to a thriving, robust atmosphere. People in barbershops and bars talked about the newest development called a subway being constructed underground. Its trains would travel the city, transporting people all over. They said one was in New York and cities in Europe.

Things were exciting, one afternoon, while getting a shave in a barbershop, the barber stopped.

"I know you. You are Jenkin Craves, one of Buck's boys."

Craves almost fell out of the chair. "Hambone? That you, Hambone? Well, I'll be. I thought you looked familiar, Hum-hum-Hambone."

Years before, the boys on the plantation kiddingly called one another one of Buck's boys. They would say, "You a Buck's boy."

The others would exclaim, "You the Buck's boy. My daddy was sold before I was born." That is what they had been told by their mothers. Buck had been a driver on work crews and administered the whip as punishment to slaves for being disrespectful or for slacking off not doing enough work.

For keeping the crews in line and producing a quota, his reward was the run of the quarters. At night, lonely women were approached with extra food and clothing in their crowded one-room cabins where the young and old stayed. Favors would eventually produce little Bucks and Buckettes. Craves began telling about things that happened.

"When we left the plantation, everybody traveled all over. Mom settled with a sister she found living outside Charleston, South Carolina. I didn't have no sisters, brothers, or halfs, I think. Except maybe you." At that, they both broke out in near-hysterical laughter.

Hambone continued, "I stayed in Mississippi for some years, saw and helped some of the old aunts and uncles. Worked around then thought I could do better up here. I tell you, it gets mighty cold in the winter, but the white folk ain't so mean."

After traveling in all those states, he had seen a tremendous amount of recently arrived immigrants from Europe. It was amazing; the country was turning all white. In the West and South their were reservations everywhere. In these parts a person would think whites were the natives.

After arriving in a small Ohio town, he finally was greeted by his longtime friend, son-in-law and the closest person to a brother he ever had. After accommodating his bags, they drove off in a one-horse buggy to the town where Joe and Shirley had settled with their budding family.

Joe brought him up on news about how Shirley's business was growing. Craves explained he had drilled new recruiters in New Mexico and Texas and participated in government operations in Wyoming, Colorado, and other territories. Joe listened in silence when he stopped speaking. Joe rode a white then said, "This is hard to explain, but there's no better time than now. Annie May—we now just call her Ann or Annie—for a while has been lacking in school."

Craves said, "That usually happens with children in their teens."

"I know," Joe said. "It happened a year back with Jim. He ran off with a circus, was gone a couple months, it liked to scare Shirley to death. Well, he came back full of stories and went back to school. He had time to make up, but seemed to not mind. Now Ann, on the other hand, is a big, big"—he was shaking his head with pity, repeating the word for emphasis—"problem. She fell in with a crowd of bad, wild kids and young grown-ups in their early twenties. Things went downhill for a bunch of them but were worst for her. Jim is a year older then her, but at sixteen and seventeen, boys and girls are a world of difference. Anyway, she had a loving fling with a smooth-talking older boy who came to town. After a while, it was found out he supplied the gang of young, adults, and older teens who hang at a known juke joint. They all started using laudanum."

"Laudanum," Craves exclaimed. "That's dope."

"It's been going around all over. It's supposed to cure everything. People that get stuck on it can't get cured. Some older boys and men beat him and ran him out of town. He ain't been seen."

After getting reacquainted with the family and seeing his young one now approaching puberty, he went to the local church and was introduced to the congregation. He was welcomed; some folks had heard of him from Sergeant Joe.

After the service, the young preacher approached and began telling what Joe wanted Craves to hear. "Me and a good friend gained information on that boy and Ann. Weeks ago, we wound up way down by the river close to Cincinnati right across from Kentucky. She had been sold to a white brawny house. We went there. They wouldn't let us in. They had a sign No Colored Allowed. From what we could see, the place was filled with common river trash. We explained who we were and why we came. A boss came surrounded by armed thugs. He told us she was sold by a black pimp. She arrived and took to their drugs like she had found heaven, smiled, and stayed high, all the time downing that stuff."

"She is young and brings in a lot of money."

We asked, "What would it take to get her back?"

He laughed. "Five hundred dollars, and that's cheap." He said, "Now she done caught a disease, but she's not losing her attractive shape and face. She is good for a couple years then out in the street she goes or she might sweep up."

Craves and Joe prepared to leave. "This is all I could get from what the preacher scrapped from the church and the money Shirley and me put together."

They put the bags in the wagon.

"Another horse is to go with us. Two is better than one. The horse will be extra. Who knows what shape she's in."

After a day, they came to a town.

"This is the place Reverend Miles told us about."

They stopped, got down, walked to a door, and knocked. The door opened. They were greeted by a big white man about forty-five to fifty years old. A badge was pinned to his shirt that showed he was in law enforcement. They discovered he also was a reverend. The house was filled with children playing. Others were held by females. They belonged to one of the many religious groups around the state.

The reverend explained, "Reverend Miles stopped a few weeks ago and told us of your plight. He had just left the place to the South. He telegraphed, you would be passing. You came at a good time. We are ready to eat."

The men looked on the plump, smiling faces of the mostly overweights. Knowing they ate well, they hurriedly joined them at a long table. An Indian woman dressed in ordinary clothes came with food.

The reverend explained, "This is our helper, Tawana. She's from the nearby reservation. She and her family come and stay a few weeks to hear words of salvation and learn English."

The woman bowed. They were served by her and the reverend's wife.

It was early afternoon when they arrived in the riverfront town. Asking around, they found the saloon were Ann was being held. It was one of many along the river where crews from boats passed, going up to Cincinnati and further south to St. Louis and on down to New Orleans. They parked the wagon in an alley on the side of the building. Then walked to the front door where they were stopped by two heavily built men.

"What y'all want? The colored places are on chapel st. Don't y'all see the sign?"

There was a big sign by the door: No Colored Allowed. Craves and Joe explained they were related to the girl Ann.

"What? Again?" one said. "Some preacher came here a couple of weeks ago. The boss talked to him. Ralph, go get Bob."

The man hurried away. Moments later, he returned. A big, fat man with a cigar stump in his mouth followed. He put his hands on his suspenders.

"Yeah, I'm Bob. I run this place. Hear y'all here for that same gal."

Joe and Craves explained, "We both raised her since she was little."

"Well, she ain't little no mo.' I paid good money to a pimp. I know you can't legally buy and sell folks no mo'! Look, I was in the Union army. I fought to free y'all. I can't help if y'all gal got with some nigger pimp and got on that laudanum stuff she loves. Now she done come down with some disease, we checked, lucky it wasn't syphilis. We cleaned her up anyway so she could keep on working. She still uses a lot of our stuff, staying in her little world. She's just money to me, she can keep doing what she wants until she can't. Nobody gonna want her in a few years anyway. Me, I'll let her clean the place. We can always get another gal to take her place."

Joe pulled a bundle open. "The preacher said you wanted $500. Nobody we know can raise that much. At the church, we raised this. And me and my missus put what we saved."

"I feel sorry for you," he said. "I'll drop it some, give me $350 and call it even.

Joe said, "We have $200 and these. They been in the family a long time." He took the silver nugget out of a pocket. They were tied in a handkerchief. Just in case more was needed, he took from another pocket two wedding rings—his wife's and her mother's.

Bob took the bundle. He and Ralph looked the things over. He said, "These rings ain't worth much. Them nuggets I gotta have appraised. I don't think that stuff is worth a hundred dollars altogether. Y'all gotta come up with another hundred. Y'all go work on one of them boats that go up and down the river. In a month, come back. Y'all will have enough."

Craves said, "We'll see." He reached for the bundle.

Bob said, "Moving away, I'll keep this as down payment."

Craves snatched the bundle from him. Joe turned to watch the others.

Angrily, Bob said, "What y'all trying to pull? I been good to you. Give a nigger an inch. He'll try to take a mile. Now get y'all black asses outta here." He grabbed at the bundled. It crashed, spilling to the wooden porch. He hollered through the door that had been cracked, "Mickey! John!"

A few men rushed from the building, putting on brass knuckles and pulling hidden blackjacks. Joe and Craves were surrounded by half a dozen men. The fight was on. With foreign objects, the men soon subdued the two. Craves raised from the floor and backed to a wall. The men moved forward.

He said, "It's a lot of y'all. Give me an even chance."

One man asked, "What he talking 'bout, boss?"

"Give me a chance with a knife and your best man."

Mickey removed brass knuckles from one hand. "Hold it. Give us a couple of knives. Let's see what the spook can do."

Both men were given Bowie knives. They began to circle, making lunges and bluffs. Craves fell to the floor after being tripped by his opponent. Mickey tried to stomp on the fallen man. Craves grabbed his foot. The man sliced and sliced at him until he rolled away. Mickey laughed. Craves began to make moves he had learned at the Apache's camp. The man, not familiar with what he saw, was puzzled. "Spooks are known for y'all knives. I ain't seen them moves though. Where you get that stuff?"

Bob asked, "Should I stop it or add another man?" Mickey hollered no then charged, making wild passes. After a few, Craves plunged his knife into his arm.

Bob told the men standing around, "Get them and throw them in that horseshit and mud in the street."

Later in the mud, half conscious. Joe mumbled, "Did you believe anything he said?"

Craves said "no".

"Me neither," Joe agreed.

People passed—black and white. All looked. None stopped, probably seeing the same done often. An old black woman and a young boy bent down to investigate.

"I saw y'all when y'all came. I knew nothing good was coming out of it, whatever made y'all come here. I'll get some men. We'll help you to your wagon."

A few black men came and helped them up and to their wagon. They recuperated in two days at the woman's house.

After hearing why they had come, they were told, "I go over there and clean up sometimes. I know Ann. She done been there over a month. I feel sorry for her. Seems by her talk she comes from good people. Said she went to school and everything. I wondered how she wind up in such a place. I see she like that stuff they addict people to. She said she was real sorry, but would never go home. She is too ashamed of the way she done turned out. What y'all gonna do now?"

Craves asked, "Who were the men who helped us?"

"Two are my boys."

Joe asked, "Where is the telegraph office?"

Craves and Joe both sawed off a piece of shotguns propped on chairs. When they finished, Craves said, "We will gladly send money for your property."

Her son Jeff said, "We gonna be waiting. They are our hunting guns. We need them to put food on the table."

Joe said, "We'll send more. You can buy those or maybe a Winchester."

The two looked, wide-eyed. "A Winchester. *Wow*. A Winchester."

"We wish we could go with you. We gotta stay here."

"Who knows what them crooks will do. Everybody knows they pay off the law. Besides, the women steal men's money. The goons rob them and throw them where we found y'all."

Craves asked. "Now where you say they keep her?"

The woman began. "Well, she's the only colored there right now . . . see."

Joe and Craves pulled up and left the wagon a few yards from the side door of the saloon. The hour was late. Most people inside were good and drunk. Some slept leaning on tables. Some played cards. A black man swept the floor. Women sat with men or roamed, looking for customers to roll for what they could get.

Both men walked through the side door, carrying a saw off shotgun in one hand and a pistol in the other. Entering, they were met by stares from customers. The bouncer surprised and the bartender reached for weapons. Craves ran and grabbed the bartender's before he could bring it into play.

Joe hollered, "First one wants to be blown apart, try something." He moved the shotgun back and forth, pointing. Another man pulled at what he thought would save the night.

Joe pointed up and blew down the chandelier. It crashed simultaneously with a bang that accompanied explosions of cross fire that coincided. That moment, the brothers came through the door both with pistols blazing, they took cover. Craves had ducked behind turned-over furniture. He scooted to them. "I thought you couldn't get involved because y'all live here."

"It's dark," one said. "They can't see us."

"If they did, they can't tell the different from us and a lot fake. Mom said y'all need help, and she didn't raise no cowards. Mom said she's in a back room upstairs."

The man who swept the place hid in a corner. The gunfight less overwhelming still continued. Craves and the brother he'd talked to ran upstairs, then began to look into the rooms. They stood to the side after knocking. Two bullet came through the door to answer.

"This is where Mom said she was." the young man said.

"Cover me," Craves knocked then jumped to the side of the door, bullets passed through the door. He crashed in and fell on the floor, pistol aimed, and saw a white male's behind fleeing through an open window. It disappeared. The frightened man had jumped to the ground. Ann lay naked on the bed in a stupor.

The boy said, "I'm strong. I'll take her." He threw a blanket over her and put her over his shoulder.

"Let's go." Craves stood guard. Gunfire downstairs now was sporadic. They knew they didn't have much time. They descended the staircase. The customers had gone, even the one who had been asleep.

"We can't go the way we came," Joe said.

The four darted from the building, blasting first with the double barrels. They ducked behind what they could find and reloaded the doubles while taking aim and firing with pistols. Each time they fired the doubles, the shots tore in the side of the building or open space. The bouncers made sure not to be in the open to receive none. They ran through the alley, put Ann in the wagon, one said, "We gonna wait for them Winchesters or go hungry. Best of luck. We've known these alleys since kids. They ain't gonna catch us."

The wagon took off, with Craves driving. They reached the end of town.

"What you doing, Joe?" he asked.

"They gonna follow. Let's use an Apache trick." A sheriff passed at the lead of a posse. The men both held the noses of one of the horses.

"I wonder how far they done got," one of the posse said. Craves held the reins as he trotted along. "I hope the stuff the lawman preacher friend gave us don't get hot while we bouncing over the place."

"It's covered but should stay cool."

After a few hours trotting, they heard galloping.

The men lashed the horses. "Kikia, Kikia, giddyap."

"It's too far to use these scatterguns, and they know pistols won't reach. Let's see what they think about the preacher's presents."

Joe moved to the back of the wagon. Ann was still asleep. "Give me some <u>always lights</u>." Craves reached into his pocket and passed <u>everywhere strike matches</u>.

"We only got six sticks of that stuff."

"Take your time and space them. They don't know how many we have."

Joe lit and threw the first dynamite stick, as expected it landed a distance in front of the posse. They stopped. The stick exploded.

"Where in hell they get that," one of them asked. "Hold up and see what they got." The wagon gained distance.

Like playing cat and mouse, a contest began, with each side using time to slow and rest their mounts. It took hours for the last stick to be thrown. Craves hashed the horses.

"Now it's us they're after, not Ann."

"You know what they'll do if we're caught."

"Don't remind me."

"It's been a good journey with you, Sarge," Joe said.

"For me too, corporal." We get caught.

"Nobody will know what happened to us."

It started raining.

"We gotta slow them."

"They have the same problem with their horses slipping," Joe said.

"They are persistent. I hope the reverend got our message. Ahead looks dry like it never rained."

They reached the dry ground and took off like bees were after them, only they were followed by something deadlier. The posse reach dry ground then let their horses run wide open.

"Get ready with them pistols when they get close. If I get hit, let go with those scatters. Fill them with buckshot and take as many as we can with us."

Galloping, they passed a sign, Shady Grove, and continued. The posse suddenly drew to a halt. The reverend sheriff with his men blocked the road. Craves and Joe had just passed when the posse arrived.

"Let us by, y'all stopping justice." "Them coons done stole one of Big Bob's gals." We gonna teach them a lesson."

The reverend's lawman said, "I'm law here. I'll do my job. And by the way, I don't particularly like <u>Big Bob</u> or the place he run now y'all turn around go back and tell him that."

CHAPTER 19

Annie Mae returned to Ohio, a physical and mental wreck. Her emotional state as an addict could only be satisfied by the drugs she craved. Ashamed of the prostituting life of her past, nightmares were common. Withdrawal shakes frightened everyone. Her sister, Shirley, had limited experience growing up on the family homestead, then marrying young. Older people around had seen detoxication before—sweating, vomiting, and other things associated with the sad, sorry affair. Superstitious farmers could only imagine she had been cursed or was the victim of voodoo. After weeks of herbs and tonics along with people praying, she began returning slowly to normal. Her drug use had been short; that made her recovery less time-consuming but still lots of agony.

After months of recuperation, she began receiving visits from her former boyfriend, after refusing to see him at first in her devastated state. A romance eventually rekindled. The father of the boy, Howard Washington, Ton was furious. The boy's understanding mother, on the other hand, helped cultivate the development. She remembered Annie growing from a little girl. After graduating high school, she didn't have to look for a job. Her sister's seamstress business was doing well, growing up, she had helped her mother and sister. With the encouragement of her family, she returned to church, The day she arrived, the service had started. That way, conversations with members were avoided. The family accompanied her. Jim, a year older, was going on twenty and was engaged. He worked at a sawmill. They all tried to enter as quietly as possible. Reverend Miles, still the preacher, saw them and continued till he finished. Afterward, the choir sang. He returned to the podium.

"Sisters and brothers, this is a special occasion. I want to personally invite one of our revered members back to the fold. Everyone knows who I am talking about. Gossip has been nonstop for months. It must stop. Ms. Annie Mae Johnson, will you please stand."

She stood. He clapped and was joined by the congregation. When clapping subsided, he continued. "Like a lost sheep, she has returned. And like our Savior said, 'Let the one or ones without sin throw the first stone.'" After a few moment, he said, "Now you can sit, sister. I didn't see anyone attempting to throw anything. There are no stones. You all get the message. I don't expect nosey people to stop being nosey. Gossiping is part of some people's nature. Try to keep it at a minimum. It might hurt some of y'all mouth doing so." People laughed. "Remember, don't bring bad luck on yourselves. The same could happen to one of your's. Thank you. There's a reunion after service. Enjoy yourselves."

Picnic tables sat outside the church. Plates of food were served by women. The congregation conversed and ate at the table with Annie's family. Howard, now twenty, approached, took his cap off, and held it to his chest. "Good afternoon, Mr. Joe, Ms. Shirley."

They were on one side of the table with their younger children. Annie, Jim, Helen—now sixteen—and others were on the other side. He waved to them then continued. "I would like to speak to you later about Ann, Mr. Joe."

Annie blushed. Joe said, "Go on."

Howard continued. "I would formally like to ask, Can I take her out sometimes?"

Joe said, "Thanks, Howard. Man to man, I don't have any objection." He looked at Shirley. "She's your younger sister. Do you have a problem with it?"

She smiled. "No. I'll be happy for you and Ann."

Two years later, Ann Mae Johnson became Ann Mae Washington. The community that had attended their church came to the ceremony. Tears flowed when they were pronounced man and wife. Joe, being the man of the house, gave the smiling bride's hand to the equally smiling, happy groom. The reception was held at his large family's house occupied by his parents and other family. The marriage was consummated in the bed he had slept in since early adulthood.

Ann, twenty, and Howard, twenty-two, spent their honeymoon traveling by train to visit relatives in Alabama. The family had been lucky enough to buy land at a discount and become owners. The nearest school of higher learning was Tuskegee Institute. Its founder and president was not related to the Washingtons of Ohio. He was a famous author of the best-selling autobiography up from slavery. The institute was gaining fame for investigations and experiments with agriculture by its resident chemist, George Washington Carver. The couple went to see another family member in the near state, Mississippi. Before they left to return home, they saw a sign that said, "Nigger, don't be seen after dark." They had heard about it; nothing like it had been seen in Ohio.

The couple returned to Ohio and their regular routines. Ann helped her sister with the business; they returned to his family home. He was too young to make foreman but advanced with the help of a smart young man who studied civil engineering at the local college. Evenings, weekends, and summers, the student was Sherman Gilmore. After a few months, to everyone's delight, Ann announced her pregnancy. The Washingtons, already grandparents of their older children's kids, welcomed the new arrivals.

Ann continued working. The sisters were soon joined by their younger sister, Barbara, was born late to their mother, Barbara. She finished school and was romantically involved with a young man everyone thought a good prospect for a lasting relation. A baby was soon born to Ann. The couple was congratulated by both families. A few months later, like many newly married, she expected another child.

CHAPTER 20

Craves thought about what Joe said years before. Poor people were getting rid of privileged blue bloods. Bombings and assassinations were happening all over the world. Newspapers fed a war fever daily. Headlines printed bold letters. Shrinking of the Main the brutal empire, crushing poor people in the Caribbean must be stopped. Colonialism in the Western hemisphere is over. We, a new democracy, must help developing people fight for liberal independence and freedom. Troops over the country were mobilized trains carried then to Tampa, Florida, and New Orleans, Louisiana. Jenkins Craves, now a master sergeant, took the one to Tampa to embark for the island of Cuba. He talked to young soldiers. Their demeanor, fresh to the army, impressed him.

"Where are you fellers from?"

One spoke up. "Ohio."

The sarge, of course, had been in touch with the now sergeant of the reserves and his wife. They raised the children he had with his beloved Barbara. They worked in their chosen trades, the boy at first thought of following his father and adoptive father, but not wanting to be a soldier and traveling, he stayed at home. Annie Mae married, stayed home, and had children of her own. He visited from time to time and was glad to see she had recovered. The danger and near death he and Joe experienced was worth the price. He stood, reminiscing a moment.

"Ohio. I have good friends there. My stepson—more like a brother—and Shirley, his wife. The younger ones still carry their mother and father's name, Johnson."

"Yes, sir, of course. He was one of my instructors, taught military science. His wife, Shirley, and the family invited me to their house and sometimes to picnics."

"I'm glad to meet you," Craves said. "They are like family. I'm Master Sergeant Jenkins Craves. I'm Private Sherman Galmore."

"I heard plenty about you, sir."

Craves thought to correct him. Sergeants are not called sir, but then at his age, he showed respect. And they were not in a formal atmosphere. The train hurried along.

"Sherman, seems a lot of people are named after the general."

"Yes, sir."

"He was a great man. Broke the back of the Confederates."

Craves thought (mum.)

"In many ways, he was. The sergeant told us about when you both rescued Ann. Nobody else talks about it now."

"Sir, I am going to Cuba. My brother was one of the sailors on the *Maine* when it exploded."

A large crowd stood watching a parade of marching troops. Craves, strutting alone, saw a man in the crowd hollering, waving, and shouting his name. He had never been in Tampa since his youth working along the waterfront. That had been ages ago. *Who could that be?* he wondered. The man hollered, "Andrew from Arizona!"

It had been twenty years. He was one of the deserters. He marched on then told the man next to him, "Gotta go. Emergency."

The man looked puzzled at him. They had rested a few moments ago. Craves fought his way through the crowd. "Andrew! Andrew!" he shouted.

Andrew, seeing him, fought his way, extending his hand. "It's been a coon's age. Whatcha been doing?" The men shook hands and embraced.

"All these years, I thought I'd never see you again. "We came back south. Abraham went to Georgia. I went to Alabama riders got him at his place."

"I heard they had him cornered. He killed two before they got him. Of course they did what they do—shot him full of holes, strung, and burned his body then paraded it. They celebrate like wild demons. Another time, some almost got me. I got away. You can see, that night, I snuck back and sniped one from some bushes. I guess I'm not so brave." If they were after you, and you knew what they were going to do, you were smart and brave."

"Yes. You were smart and brave!" Craves repeated. "All these years, you ever hear from the military? No, I hope I never will. They let them crackers pick us up and work us almost to death on them chain gangs. I've been working as a seaman, been all over. All down South America. In Asia, I went to China and a bunch of places. I've even been to Africa. Yeah, I've been over there a few times. Saw all kinds of stuff. The people speak a bunch of languages I couldn't understand. I found out, some of those kings been fighting their asses off. In a place called Sudan, one called the Mahdi destroyed a whole British army. In another place close to them, named Ethiopia. You heard about it. It is in the Bible. Their king Malike destroyed a twenty thousand–man Italian army. They kicked ass all over in a place I hate, <u>South Africa</u>. They like down here in the South—treat colored bad. But a long time ago, over fifty years, Shaka, king of the Zulu, beat the hell out of a bunch of British."

"You woulda thought it was Custer's last stand." They both laughed. "I still sail, but not as much because I play trumpet in one of them new bands. They call the music jazz. It's a lot of fun. Everybody plays their hearts out. If you ever come back, I changed my name to Charlie. You know why? Just come around the colored section around the river, ask for Charlie the trumpet player. You'll find me. Lots of them good-looking gals too."

Craves smiled. "You don't say." The parade, still passing, was finishing. Craves said goodbye and ran to get his spot and get on the ship heading for Cuba. Before they left there was a racial disturbance - it was quelled by the Army tore itself apart.

Arriving in Cuba, Craves knew the army and marines were going to do the brunt of the fighting. A newly organized company called Rough Riders were untried in battle, but getting a lot of attention, the name implied a hearty group. Some of the men had ridden the range in the West as wranglers and cowboys during the last cattle drives across Kansas, Oklahoma, and Texas; they were indeed rough. The military hadn't seen action in many years. Those had been against hostile tribes decades ago. Those scrimmages and engagements were mostly by hit-and-run guerrilla bands. There were on hand so many newsmen they seemed to make a small army.

Being a hardened, seasoned veteran, Craves knew he was responsible for the welfare of his mostly young men. Standing in line at attention, he told them. "Men, take orders only from our officers and noncoms. Let the glory seekers seek glory but not at our expense."

They left the ships at thirteen miles east of Santiago, then the Cuban capital, strutting to their camp. The horses didn't disembark.

The men, not accustomed to foreign customs, were surprised to see the Cuban army. The scourge of slavery there had ended about a decade earlier. The stigma didn't seem to apply. The officers corps was integrated black officers and Noncom's led their army. Of course, that didn't happen in the Spanish army. The Spanish overseas empire that lasted four hundred years was about to end. In that century, it had lost all its South American and Central American colonies. The largest was Mexico. Now it stood to lose the ones in the Caribbean and Far East, the Philippines and Guam. The new rising world power promised to rule with strength, but rule fairly, regardless of color, religion, or status of birth. That promise was being met with optimism. One thing for sure— whatever happened would bring big changes.

A white officer rejoined the Tenth. He had served with it during his first assignment after graduating West Point during the Indian Wars of the 1880s. His name was Black Jack Pershing. He was called Black Jack because of his close association with black troops. A decade and a half later, he would lead the punitive expedition into Mexico to catch and punish General Francisco Pancho Villa. After he attacked the armory at the Columbus New Mexico's, where he and his five hundred–man strong army burned the town, killing American citizens and taking arms. Read book *Buffalo Soldiers: South of the Rio Grande* by yours truly.

General Pershing led the American forces in France during World War I. Later, he became the highest-ranking general of the US with Four gold stars he was general of the army.

CHAPTER 21

The US Goes To War In The Philippines

Black troops trained and waited at the presidio in California to be dispatched for action. In Cuba, Major Charles Young was the highest-ranked colored.

Colored press, such as the Indianapolis Freeman, on March 18, 1898, said in an editorial, "If the government wants our service let US demand protection at home, Aganish Lynchings." Something that was becoming common.

Some press viewed the coming war as American imperialism.

Dr. Booker T. Washington spoke negatively, "Black going to fight colored people is no progress. The government should be ashamed to have Colored Troops participate."

The same tune was repeated by most activists of the day. W. E. B. Du Bois and Ida B. Wells, journalists and activists who wrote about blacks' conditions in the South, both stated conditions in Asia and Africa for dark- and light-skinned people were on the threshold of change, American blacks should be at the forefront of that change.

For the government like in Cuba, the idea of the time was colored were better suited for the tropics and could therefore better fend off diseases of those regions like yellow fever, typhoid, and malaria.

Previously in Cuba, the men had been honored as brave and received a large welcome in a parade down Fifth Avenue when they returned.

It was known that they did a considerable amount of fighting on the famous hill that ended land combat and saved a lot of rich Rough Riders Lives. The only person to badmouth them was the man who wanted all the glory for his outfit and himself, the future president.

He stated Negro troops were slackers in their duties and would only go as far as they were led by white officers. Most other white officers disagreed with the statement.

There was much controversy in 1899 about occupying the newly obtained Philippines.

The country's the 350-year rule had always been contested by the islanders. Their geography made cohesiveness, an almost insurmountable problem. There were seven-thousand-plus islands with varied customs, and languages. The latest large organized resistance in the North wanted complete independence, not an exchange of Spanish rulers for American. The leader was an educated man named Emilio Aguinaldo.

Spanish culture had been adopted and thrived in the capital city, Manila, and was well entrenched in many large islands. In those, the people spoke Spanish and had become Catholics and were mixed Filipino and Spanish blood.

The US had decided the islands would be administered by experienced professionals who held the welfare of the islanders in regard.

The US expected to be welcomed as liberators. None expected to be met by a beehive like the first Spaniard had 350 years earlier. They were met by aggressive fighters. The Spanish leader, Ferdinand Magellan, was decapitated by a fierce tribal chieftain, named Lapu-Lapu.

A reason the US wanted the islands, besides commerce and military strategic purposes, was other growing powers in the region would take them for those purposes. Mainly Germany and Japan. The Imperial powers in the region had for years been content with their colonies. The British had Malaysia, France, Indochina, Indonesia, was controlled by the Dutch.

The prevailing liberal idea in the States was why assault a indefensible racial group who were trying to obtain self-determination. A counter opinion wanted to avoid occupying islands that were colored whether in the Caribbean or Asia and assimilate them. Their idea was to have open-door immigration from Europe.

President William McKinley and his vice president, Theodore Roosevelt, chose the strategic reason. It was thought young factory workers in the North with jobs that show little future advancement would see the military as a chance to escape. Poor whites who worked sharecropping in fields with their parents would be glad to escape for adventure. The same was considered for colored in those positions.

A Convoy of American troop ships accompanied by large and small warships left for the Far East. The newest battleships, cruisers, and destroyers had arrived weeks earlier and destroyed the Spanish fleet in Manila Bay. To the dismay of the local people who had fought many years, the US paid the Spanish $20,000,000 to leave. It was an insult. The money could have helped the suffering Filipinos. They felt because they were dark, the white combatants cared little of their opinion. When the US began a dialogue with Emilio, their leader, he couldn't be gratified.

When the troops arrived, there were seven thousand whites and three thousand coloreds. Knowing the controversy that raged about coloreds fighting oppressed people of color, their units were sent mostly to pacified areas, though the final consensus was that if the coloreds wanted to be citizens, they couldn't choose the wars they would fight.

The white army were enthused with the prevailing idea. Nonwhites were the white man's burden and had to be civilize. *Slant-eyed nigger* was a slang often used.

The coloreds followed their time-proven habit when meeting new people—with ways they did not understand.

Smiles showed a desire to help. This many had learned, while stationed on reservations where Native Americans had been defeated.

Attack on the Moros in the south were met with such ferocity a powerful new weapon had to be invented. Armed with bolos— twisted knives—charging Moros would keep advancing, after being shot several times and skillfully dispatch, his opponent, in their case, an American soldier. The .45 Automatic's <u>kick</u> was invented for the purpose of knocking them backward.

The death rate for the US rose to four thousand and many wounded. Their combatants along with civilians, rate was ten times more. Tropical diseases overwhelmed many, as prophesied. What also had been forewarned fighting savage people (people with different values) on their land would become a no-bars slide into savagery. Each side would begin to retaliate with stronger actions. The US, not able to control things, would get a black eye around the world.

Because all the people looked alike, supposed no-kill zones were set for friendly noncombatants. Meanwhile, an infamous general named Jacob H. Smith, out of desperation, unbelievably ordered <u>kill all males in kill zones over ten years old</u>—old enough to hold a weapon to defend their land. The unfortunate order was not enforced. Instead, the general himself came under attack and was court-martialed. His record was checked. During the American Civil War, he had come under fire different times for money fraud, when he had used colored soldiers as shields for his activities. Before the Geneva Convention, the code was called Lieber Code. It permitted killing POWs in reprisals and saboteurs and guerrilla fighters on the spot.

At trial, the general stated the present fighting was like the fights against American Indians. President T. Roosevelt intervened and retired the general without punishment.

William Howard Taft was governor of the Philippines. John Pershing, then a captain, used irregular tactics—no massacres but befriended local elders and learned dialects on the island of Samar the Spanish had never conquered. The Moros, in hot area, wore scant garments. When the Americans came, the chaplains, Catholic or Protestant, wanted the women to wear petticoats. The soldiers soffed let them wear what they want. The women and girls, both friendly, romanced and made love freely with those of their choosing. Soon, many were attacked and gang raped. The men, not willing to stop when they thought they had been encouraged, were sometimes uncontrollable. The locals, being a different type of Muslim, were hard to understand. Captain Connell in command tried to accommodate the feelings of both groups. The Moros secretly raided and killed fifty-nine. It was called the Balangiga Massacre. The biggest massacre of army soldiers since the Battle of the Little Bighorn in 1876. The Philippines complained that Americans burned whole towns on the island in revenge.

The men under Captain Wolf's command, which included Sherman Gilmore and Joe Jr. of the Ohio National Guard, David Fagen and half a dozen colored soldiers, ran toward a building scheduled to be blown up. People inside were unaware and did not speak the dialect of the translators.

They had entered during the night for shelter. It now was appearing day. The officer in charge of the white troop near heard what had happened. A group of his men rose in response. The commander ordered, "Remain here." The men didn't obey and continued toward. The commander hollered, "Don't help them nigger chinks." He fired his pistol into the air. "Grumbling chink lovers gotta be a bunch of Yankees. Damn it."

David Fagen, Joe, and Gilmore entered the house. Time was running out. They saw a group of frightened women with children huddled in corners. David, with more field experience, explained in Spanish and all the dialects he could rattle off what was happening. The women, now understanding, grabbed children and ran. The men follow them outside. The group of white soldiers arriving helped with the children and ran like crazy. Getting a few hundred feet. The house went up with a large explosion.

STORIES OF THE AFRICAN AMERICAN FRONTIER CALVARY *113*

Fifteen soldiers deserted while in action. Six were black. David Fagen became a famous captain in the Philippine army. A 600 dollar 25 thousand-dollar todays money—was placed on this head by the US. It was collected by a Filipino who defected from the rebels. The Philippines claimed the head to be someone else. David Fagen faded into legend as a Zorro-type figure. People claimed he got married, raised a family, and lived in the surrounding hills and jungle.

Later, Emilio Aguinaldo made peace and worked with the Americans for the betterment of his people.

CHAPTER 22

Gilmore

To most people, Monica looked white. She was from the island of Martinique. The administration at her school were aware of her mixed blood. Other French-speaking Creols, mostly from Louisiana, studied there.

Sherman and Monica were horse enthusiasts. During their leisurely time, while riding, they were often looked at curiously by people from both races. When Sherman decided to take her home to meet his family, they tried to discourage the relation, saying nothing good would come of it. Monica and him were not dissuaded. They were young educated full of spirit and ready to accept the challenge of the new century. She wrote to her family of her intentions to marry a soldier of the New Colored Officers Corps. The family was furious. Her father was white. Her mother was Creole. The family had had a tradition of marrying only white or nearly white people of French ancestry. The tradition had been followed in most French and Spanish islands; a separate class had developed. The ruling Europeans created it through blood relations; it was maintained for generations. The largest of the French island's Haiti had been the scene of a bloody slave rebellion when former slaves massacred the plantation owners. The remaining owners fled to other islands or north to the Louisiana territory. Telegraphs were busy transmitting messages back and forth from her island to remind her of her obligation. Even though she was an adult, she had a social position. And her personal dowry was ready to be given to someone of her class.

After months passed, a compromise was made. One of her brothers came to accompany them to her home. The Catholic Church would not marry persons of different faiths. On their island, they were wealthy, and had made arrangements with the archbishop for special considerations in their case. Her dowry of £50,000 or equal in Spanish pieces of eight (used in international trade at the time).

The money a century later would translate in $2,500,000 dollars. Each of her siblings received the same.

The social climate presented a situation that was similar in most parts of the world at that time. There was only one independent black country in Africa, Ethiopia, and one in the Western hemisphere, Haiti. Brazil was half black but the ruling class was of European descent.

Andre Aristotle Ledet was twenty-five. He spoke French and some English. His appearance fit the description of an aristocratic South American. Well dressed, he carried himself with an air of importance and was obviously well-off. Carrying a French passport, he was accepted in places dark-skinned persons only worked. After traveling by ship, he arrived in Ohio on a train where he had bought a private berth. He met his sister at her residence in town. They both went to meet Sherman and this family at their home.

It was a warm Saturday afternoon. Monica was slightly nervous; she wanted her brother to like her fiancé. Sherman's father was a wounded Union soldier during the Civil War. His mother had been a slave. They were both deceased. Sherman came out of the house. He was greeted with a warm "Bonjour, I am Andra Artistole Ledet." He extended his hand and gave a slight bow of his head. The action showed some military school background.

While shaking hands, Sherman said, "Monica told me you speak some English."

"Yes, I do."

At that moment, two of Sherman's brothers came from the house, wanting to see and meet their brother's soon to be brother-in-law. After engaging in small talk, they all rode around town in a large two-horse-drawn buggy. Cars were new. There were only a few on the road, especially in the country. Andre stayed at a small expensive hotel in town.

The trio began their journey. Complications didn't begin until they crossed the Mason-Dixon line. In those days, the Plessy versus Ferguson law had been in effect less than a decade. Crossing it, coloreds and whites were segregated. No stipulation had been made for Native Americans and Orientals. Sherman was wearing his uniform like most military men did in those days. The Ledets, with their foreign passports, were able to travel first class in private berths.

Sherman was accommodated in a compartment for well-off colored people. Avoiding discomfort, they rode a train to Tampa, Florida; disembarked; boarded a merchant ship; and continued their journey. Sherman changed into his tropical uniform. The ship was one of many that doubled as transport for passengers and cargo that loaded and unloaded at various ports around the Caribbean. The Ledet family's enterprises, included ownership of some of those ships. Andre went to the bridge to speak with the captain whom he knew. Eventually, they arrived in Martinique. They were met by a horse-drawn carriage. Soon they passed plantations where dark laborers worked in sugarcane fields. Under a hot tropical sun, some of them stopped and waved as they passed. They arrived at a mansion. People were standing and sitting on the veranda. Others were just arriving on horseback or on carriages. The carriage stopped. Everyone stepped off. Monica gave Sherman her hand. He picked her up at her waist and put her on the ground. Some of the onlookers gasped at what was considered over endulance and improper handling of a woman not yet his wife. A new convertible car sped to a squeaking stop in front of the house. A young man, about twenty, jumped out. He hurried up the steps where he hugged and kissed on the cheek a medium-size white man about sixty years old then kissed a dark, shorter woman who was in her late forties. Sherman, Monica, and Andre walked up the five steps. The man, Monica's father, hugged and kissed his daughter. She then bent and kissed her mother. Sherman approached.

She said, "Papa, meet my fiancé."

The man shook his hand, kissed him on both cheeks, then said, "Bonjour, hello."

Sherman moved to the lady. Monica said in French, "Mama, mi fiancé Sherman Gilmore." The father said, "I am Counti Frances Frasso Portier Duvalier Ledet. You can forget the Counti part—it was a title of my family before the revolutions. Many of my relatives lost their heads over it. I keep it as a remembrance only. He stepped back a ways, looked inquiringly at him, and said, "So you are the prince who has dazzled my princess. You want her to denounce money and marry a soldier yourself in the officers corps. You have charmed my princess and will take her from me?"

Sherman said, Sir . . . Monsieur Conti Frances, your daughter will always be your daughter. I want to make her my wife."

Conti Frances said, "Call me Monsieur Ledet please. You can see by my family I have passed convention and have established the family I want."

He, of course, was referring to his mixed-race family. It had been a fact in all the colonies that every European power ruled the upper class and lower class had mixed first with the Native Americans and then the slaves brought from Africa. New hues of color developed Mulllato half and half quadroon an Octoroon half quadroon and white. What the count meant about his family was that he married and recognized his wife as his legal mate whereas others did not. His wealth gave him the privilege of not caring what the general population thought about him and his family.

Sherman was introduced to all family members present. The wedding was announced. The mansion had as many as thirty rooms. Some were for servants and guests. Monica had her room. Sherman was given one on another floor a distance away in the three-story house. To discouraged his night prowling. In less than a month, the couple would have to return to their lives in Ohio. Wedding plans were made.

The Ledet's large extended family were administrators in the local bureaucracy. The government was run by locally born Frenchmen. Slavery had been abolished in all the Caribbean islands earlier in the previous century. Guadelopue, one of the neighboring French islands, was the birthplace of a renowned general, the father of the famous author of *The Three Musketeers, The Man in the Iron Mask*, and *The Count of Monte Cristo*, Alexandre <u>Dumas</u>. Martinique, Napoleon's wife Josephine was born there. The hot sun beat down on the large mansion. In front and on the sides, long tables were draped with beautifully embroidered tablecloths, groups of people sat. The family had their tables. On the other side of the house, workers gathered; it was a Sunday. All were there to celebrate the wedding. It had been held inside the family house. There was a compromise. Sherman, a non-Catholic, could not be married in the local cathedral. A priest had held the wedding at the Ledets' house. After much feasting and fireworks, everyone left the gala event and went home. The bride and groom retired to the bridal suite.

After a night of fulfilling their commitment, the newlyweds awoke late. The family was being served breakfast downstairs. The couple was greeted by everyone. Two of her brothers had studied English and greeted Sherman in English. Monsieur Ledet said in French, "I see you didn't perform the traditional ritual." He paused. "Well, since you are an adult, it doesn't have to be enforced."

Her mother stood quietly, her head slightly bent.

Monica said, "I didn't bring down the sheets, and I am not ashamed. If anyone wants to go check if there is blood, they are welcome to look."

"Don't worry," the father said. "When they change the bed, the servants will see. Then everyone on the island will know."

Everyone laughed. Sherman did not understand. He hunched his shoulders and continued to look at everyone and then at her.

She said, "You are a big part of the topic," then explained the tradition.

He laughed and said, "Monsieur and family, I'm sure you will be pleased when you examine our sheets and what you will discover."

The father asked Andre to translate. Everyone afterward nodded their approval. Monica's mother stood, walked to her daughter, and gave her a big hug and kiss. Happy she did not let the family down and still had remained a virgin, until after the ceremony.

Monsieur Ledet then said, "What we agreed to still stands, your dowry will go to your husband if he stays and makes Martinique his home. On your thirty-fifth birthday, it will go to you wherever you are. There are problems for coloreds everywhere. I hope the future will change. For now, you have a well-established family here. It's your choice. At your age, you think money isn't everything, but believe me, it is. That is money and family." He held out his hands and gestured, saying in French, "It's everything. You will soon see. Money ah--Magnifique."

"You, monsieur." He rose from the table and walked over to Sherman. "Please stand." Sherman stood. He hugged then kissed both his cheeks.

Stepping back, he reached into his front pocket. From it, he withdrew a thick envelop as large as a small package. He gave it to him. He said, "For many years, I thought I would be giving this to the Le Blancs on the other side of the islands. They are distant family who have many able unmarried young men. But my daughter chose you like I chose her mother. I wish you both the best of luck. I am sure you will be more than satisfied with the finances for your honeymoon. I have sent a cable to a bank in your hometown to help you get started. A soldier's pay is not what I want my daughter to live on."

Sherman was surprised at the generous amount he had been given. It was more money than he had made in his entire life. There was, of course, a stipulation attached. He was not surprised. The old man always had some accompanying reason behind whatever he did. The agreement was that he and his wife would accompany her brother on a business trip to South America. It was decided that while traveling, he would wear civilian clothing. There was a lot of anti-Yankee feeling expressed where he was going.

Andre was going to be representing the family business. He carried pocket money. The large gift his father had given Sherman was put into Andre's personal account. Money would be withdrawn for all their expenses as the occasions arose.

Rio de Janeiro was a large bustling and growing city by the Atlantic Ocean. It reminded Sherman of large cities in the states because he saw so many black people. If he had not been close enough to hear them speaking, he would have thought he was in New York or Chicago. Like the US, at the time, many European immigrants were arriving to take advantage of the booming economy. Local Natives were being displaced or slowly disappearing into the melting pot of races. Brazil had been a Portuguese colony during colonial time. It was settled over a hundred years before Jamestown in Virginia and before the pilgrims landed at Plymouth Rock. It had the largest black population imported from Africa. The group spent days sightseeing some on beaches; other times, they went to places where money determined the clientele. Most of the time, Sherman was at a lost. He didn't speak Portuguese, Spanish, or French. His companions eagerly translated for him. Contacts and contracts with businesses were completed. They continued to Colombia, where business was to be completed. Afterward, they would separate. Andre would go to his home, Sherman and Monica to theirs. They boarded a train for the port city of Cartagena. The long ride took days. It was hot and tedious. They rode through jungles and across mountains. The honeymoon had been a pleasant experience. Sherman's travel experiences had been extensive but limited to military affairs with the army, never with any convenience and never with the company of a woman. They were inconvenienced, but traveled first class with the luxury that class extended.

"We will soon return to our normal routines—me managing the plantation and both of you, your occupations." Andre was melancholy. The train had traveled forty miles an hour. Suddenly, it began to halt.

Sherman said, "I wonder what's happening."

At that moment, pistol shots were heard. Looking out the window, he saw that one side of the train ran close to a mountain. On the other side, there was a gravel road thirty feet wide to its edge. A cliff made a drop of hundreds of feet down. A group of about fifteen men rode on the gravel path, each firing into the air. Porters ran excitedly through the aisle, waving their hands.

"Please, everybody, please be calm. There is a robbery. The soldiers may come soon. That would be more dangerous. They will shoot at one another. The robbers will leave but someone may get hurt." He stuttered. "I . . . I mean, some of the passengers."

The train only had seven cars carrying passengers. Trains that carried cargo were sometime twenty to thirty cars long. The front then the back doors smashed open with a bang. Four men carrying guns rushed through both. Some had pistols; others carried rifles. Sherman noticed two in one group were almost jet-black.

They hollered in Spanish, "We want all your money! This no-good train is not carrying any payroll. It doesn't have no guards." Trains carrying payroll to the miners or to banks had guards. "We do not like to rob civilians, but we have no choice. You can afford to ride a train, so all of you have money. If not, you would all be riding donkeys." He laughed. "Ain't that right?" Please stand.

His men all laughed. One of the black men had a gold tooth, which he showed with his broad smile. Everybody stood. There were about twenty people onboard. Some were women with a few children; most were men. The robbers moved quickly through the compartment, taking men's and women's rings, pocket watches, snatching pageants and chains from the women's necks. All of these put into sacks they carried. Other men threw suitcases and luggages around from overhead ricks. On the floor, searched each thoroughly. Religious articles and statues the bandits eagerly took. All the time, they were moving and hollering, "Quickly *vamos* quickly! *Vamos!*"

Stopping at Sherman and his group, the black man with the gold tooth said in Spanish, "What do we have here?" "Black man, you got money?"

At that moment, the luggage from overhead was lowered and opened. Monica's wedding dress was removed. They held it up. The uniform and other properties were stored and locked in a special compartment. Looking at the dress, the gold-toothed man said, "Good, hum, just what I need for my senorita, but no, it might bring bad luck."

He hunched. He didn't understand. Monica said, "He is my husband."

Andre said, "And my brother-in-law."

The man looked and saw Andre's watch and reached for it. Andre unlocked the watch from his belt and gave it to him. He saw Monica's gold band and reached for it. "Where you people come from?"

Andre said, "Me and my sister are from the islands of Martinique." He pointed to Sherman. "He is from the US."

The man exclaimed, "A Yankee. I've never met a black Yankee."

He held out his hand. "You have money, black Yankee? I need it for my poor family. You are maybe not rich, but you ride a fancy train."

Sherman pulled out a few British pounds and handed them to the man.

He grinned and looked at the British money. "Look. I'll only take little." He took half. "I don't want black Yankees mad at me. Might be bad luck. The beautiful woman is yours. Good luck. When you get back to where you come from, tell them gringos that canal they are building through our stolen land called Panama we will take back."

The men laughed. He continued, "We are letting you build it. Then we will take it. It will be ours for free." See free.

They all laughed then left the train. A few shots were fired. They rode off.

The canal was being built in the new country of Panama, a breakaway province of Colombia. The French had tried to build one thirty years before. The scrounge of yellow fever and malaria was so bad the project was abandoned. Now it was being completed by the US on a leased zone under American protection. Black contracted workers from all over the Caribbean worked under the burning tropical sun. White men's skins would have blistered under the conditions. The work was done for wages. Their slave ancestors would have loved. Dr. Walter Reed had developed a vaccine that promised a cure for the dreaded infections.

They reached the beautiful city of Cartagena. Its markets were full of tourists who shopped and returned to cruise ships that had brought them there. They were a number of forts with large cannons protruding from them—they were a reminder of long-gone days when they protected the city from pirates and buccaneers who raided the Spanish main.

Those swashbuckling thieves had passed into history, but some of their lighthearted spirits remained in the form of train-robbing bandits.

After sightseeing and rearranging each party bade the other farewell. Andre continued home. Sherman and Monica took a ship to Jamaica then one to New Orleans. While in Jamaica, they heard of a new idea being promoted that encouraged Pan-Africanism. Its motto was "Up, you mighty race." The leader and spokesperson of the new movement was named Marcus Garvey. The movement would gain popularity in the US. Its long-term agenda was to return black people to Africa, and develop it.

New Orleans was the busy city it had always been. Sherman had never been there. Over half the people in the city spoke French. It was known for racial divisions. White people had their part of the city. Light-skinned mulattos stayed to themselves; dark-skinned people were shunned and forced to be away from the dominant society. They were the domestics and laborers. After returning to the States, Sherman wore his uniform. As he and his bride walked, they were not accosted but often stared at and whispered about. They were not a common couple, but not rare.

Passing a downtown jewelry store, he said, "This looks like a nice place." They entered. There were only a few customers. All stopped to look at them. They proceeded to the counter. A clerk said, "What can I do for you? Coloreds don't shop here. They go to Dryer Street. That's your section."

Sherman said, "We only want a wedding band."

The clerk looked confused at their obvious differences in color. He stuttered, "But . . . but . . . ." then spoke in French to another clerk. "This black man with the white woman. What the hell is happening?"

The other said, "She's probably Creole."

"I don't care. She looks white to me, and she's with this—this black scum."

Monica interrupted in French. "My husband is black but not scum. We were married on my home island, Martinique. My wedding band was lost in a robbery while we honeymooned. He is an officer and a representative of your government."

Both men apologized in French. One asked, "Your ring size please?"

After leaving New Orleans, they returned to Ohio and resumed their professions; Sherman an instructor of military science at the local college and Monica a professor of romance languages.

In the months that passed, Monica had a son. She was content being a housewife. Andre and his family visited from the island.

The next year, a daughter was born. They lived comfortably on the money she received from her father and their salaries. He became a first lieutenant and went to another assignment. The family followed. They would soon be played by an epidemic Sherman's family would perish.

CHAPTER 23

By the beginning of the 1900s, the country had gone through much change. The industrial world had produced what was called the gilded age. The megarich who lived an obstinate lifestyles attracted the attention of a new movement, the anarchist. President McKinley, not an aristocrat or blue blood as he was called by Leon Czolgosz, the zealot, his assassin who deemed he was the main representative of the society that produced the large differences in classes. The Northeast and Mid West were plagued by social unrest. Violent labor strikes became endemic and welled quelled by state national guard. The government stayed busy trust busting, stopping businesses from monopolizing the market.

A large presence of African American soldiers were still in the Philippines, the Twenty-Fourth and Twenty-Fifth Infantry and the Ninth and Tenth Cavalry.

Sergeant Major Craves had been stationed at Fort Bliss, El Paso, Texas, with other men he had been with over the years

Tecumseh and Cherokee were in the Philippines. Because of their experience on the frontier and Cuba, they were both sergeants who now spoke good English. Their wives remained in the West—El Paso was at the international crossing with Mexico, where commercial traffic passed, going both ways. A long bridge facilitated the movement that also helped a undercurrent of illicit businesses by Mexican and American outlaw gangs. The military was close to where famous bad men like John Wesley Hardin had passed their years. Now there were local sheriffs and federal marshals along with state Texas rangers. Towns and the countrysides now safe were not friendly to Mexicans or blacks, especially in East and North Texas. Mexicans and those mixed with Native Americans were numerous in the West.

One afternoon, Craves walked to company headquarters, went in, and sat. Moments later, a young lieutenant came from an office. "The major will see you now, Sergeant Major."

Craves went into the office, stood, and saluted. The major stood saluted and said, "At ease and congratulations again, Sergeant Major. I hope you are adjusting well to your new position with all its responsibilities and everything. I know it's a demanding job. Your military career has been excellent. I suggest you continue until you reach fifty-five then retire. You only have a few years left. Your pension, should be sufficient you being widowed with grown children."

Craves said, "Yes, sir. Will that be all, sir?"

"It will," the major said. They saluted.

Craves left. Walking, he thought, *Thirty-eight years is a long time*. The major said the new rank required more skills. Reading and writing for sure—things he had never gotten a good handle on. His duties involved going to the Mexican town of Juárez were transits came and went. Being close to an American city with a fort had its advantages. Every night, young soldiers streamed across the border, looking for excitement. The many cantinas and bodellos offered, of course, there were conveniences. The aftermath were fights and other mischief associated with drunken soldiers. The sarge, accompanied by US officials, did what became routine: get men out of jail. Back in the US, the soldiers might spend a few days in the fort's lockup. When released, in a short time, many repeated the same thing.

Living in a small house outside the fort, he would go to town to drink and play cards. He was the highest noncommissioned officer. Black officers had become present on various posts. One day, he and an officer who spoke Spanish saw a man who look like him while they were in Juárez. The translator questioned the man and was told he was from a town in an area in the state of Veracruz, a town named after a black prince brought from Africa during colonial time hundreds of years earlier. He led a revolution that killed many Spaniards. The man was Gaspar Yanga. Both men were surprised and hoped they would learn more. Some knew of blacks east of them in towns along the Mexican side of the border who settled there with Seminole Indians of Florida. They were invited by the Mexican government before slavery ended in the States. being aware of whatever happened; his attention was soon focused on the same as the men a new good looking. Women had come to town named Cora.

Cora had come on an unplanned visit to see an aunt and stayed.

She had had difficulty in East Texas, where she lived. Her family were sharecroppers. Like her, who migrated over South Texas. At one camp, the boss insisted she work with his wife in their house. To Cora, work was work. Now, at least she wouldn't have to be in the hot sun. The missus of the house was told by Cora that her name was Cora Mea. The woman liked Mea and would call her that. Cora insisted she be called the name she chose.

After an argument, the women continued calling her what she wanted. You mean to me. "Like it or not, you sassy baboon."

Cora punched the woman, giving her a black eye. That was a no-no in those parts, The KKK ruled. In similar instances where blacks had done what they considered an assault to a white, the person had been whipped, paraded around, and, sometimes worse. A black domestic, while working, overheard plans to punish Cora. That night, she told Cora and her family what she had overheard. Cora had two teenage daughters but no husband. The family sent the girls to a safe place. Then drove Cora to the railhead and sent her to a relative who lived on the other side of the state, El Paso.

It wasn't long before Cora became known to the local community, after she frequented bars in colored towns. Making acquaintances with soldiers, they found out what she had, she gave to men of her choosing. Some, after drinking, propositioned her. When under the influence, she might say anything maybe tell the culprit to go see his mama. Her down-to-earth, uncultured vulgarity got her the scorn of most women. She had recently fought two, who claimed she had slept with their men. Such accusations would turn into shouting matches and brawls—the brawls she always won. Afterward she would sashay off, hollering over her shoulder, "Give the man what he wants, he might stay home."

After a few weeks, a lot had been said about her. One night, she walked into the saloon, stood at the smokey bar, and drank. Some men offered to buy hers more becoming tipsy, she looked and saw Craves playing cards with a group of soldiers. When the game ended, she walked to his table.

"Hi, I'm Cora."

"Everybody knows you," he said. She ran her hand on his sleeve over his many stripes.

"Mister Sarge."

Craves said, "Yes, I'm Sergeant Major Jenkins Craves. Can I help you?"

She sat across from him in an empty chair. She pulled it close to him. "I seen you around. You mind company?"

"No, join me and have something."

She whistled. A woman approached; both ordered—Craves a beer, she a double shot of whiskey.

"We both have seen each other. I hope you haven't heard anything bad about me."

"I heard plenty. I don't pay attention to gossip," Craves said. "What do you do when you are not here? I mean, for money. I heard you don't hustle. If you did, I'm sure men would pursue you."

"I hope you would be one. I live a boring life," she said. "I live with an old aunt who spends all her time at church. I go sometimes, but it's boring. I come here to let go and have fun."

"I don't go to church myself. Maybe you can invite me sometime," he said.

"Mr. Sergeant Major, this might be a blessing. Tomorrow is Sunday, and I have had too much already. I'm going home and getting some sleep. I'll be fresh in the morning."

He said, "I was just leaving. I know where your aunt lives. I'll take you there then go home. I can pick you up in the morning."

They left the saloon.

The next day, Craves came to Cora's house, driving a one-horse carriage. They arrived at church; the congregation was small. A few soldiers in uniform nodded in respect. Nobody salutes in church. After service, he drove her home. Walking her to her door, she said, "Mr. Sarge, I haven't had such a feeling in a good long time. Hum, what a feeling."

"I enjoyed your company too. Can I call again maybe tomorrow night? We can go to the place we met. Then I'll bring you home.

She said, "Hum hum. You ain't said nothing."

They hugged and had a quick kiss.

"Oh," he said. "No more Mr. Sarge. We friends. Just call me Craves."

She smiled. "Will do," she entered the house.

After a few dates, he told her, "You have brought light into my gloomy life. Why don't you move in? It will stop me having to pick you up and bring you home. Can you cook?"

She put her hands on her hips. "Mr. Craves, you are looking at the best home cook in East Texas."

Craves retired from the army after a brief ceremony. He told her, shacking up, "Ain't nobody's business but ours. I've been married a couple of times but never been happier than now."

A year passed. He had gotten used to the woman twenty years younger than himself. She grew used to the company and security he gave. The match was joyous; the nights romantic. Both agreed they didn't need more children. His were grown; hers were in their late teens. Cora turned out to be the cook she claimed to be. Her specialty was East Texas barbecue and pan-fried corn bread, candied yams and snap beans.

The black troops had come from the Midwest and down South. The working women were from the same places.

One day, Cora gave free samples at the saloon. Afterward their place stayed busy, trying to keep up with orders. The people enjoyed food they had grown up on. Craves's pension was enough for both of them lived comfortably. She enjoyed the new earning. It was the first time she was able to accumulate money. With it, she had store-bought clothes and knickknacks to adorn the house. They saved to have inside plumbing, flush toilet, and warm water to bath. They were proud of their new gadgets like toothbrush and its accompanying toothpaste. Friends and neighbors warned about losing their protective teeth enamel. Their concern was being more sanitary and pleasant. Both shared year-old habits: she dipped snuff and he chewed tobacco.

On weekends, they served food at baseball games. White soldiers showed up to get East Texas barbecue and pan-fried corn bread.

One afternoon, they were at a picnic. Cora had been drinking. A half-drunk woman approached. "After all this time, I don't see no babies."

"That's none of your business," Cora said, still sitting at a table.

The woman continued, "I'm making it my business."

"You swishing your tail around like a hen. You ain't nothing but a dried-up old slut." Cora began pushing away from the table then stood.

The woman continued, "And that old man ain't got no more lead in his pencil."

Cora moved closer to the woman and yanked her long skirt then pulled it. The woman, completely bare from the waist down, screamed and tried covering herself. She wobbled away, "Oh my lord. Oh damn you and him."

Cora walked over to her man. "Don't pay that slut no mind, honey." She hugged him and into his ear, said, "You got plenty of lead in that pencil. I was going to tell you you've been writing good." She patted her stomach. "Yeah, about three months."

"Oh my god!" he yelled. "You mean—"

She nodded her head yes. "Well, honey, no more drinks."

He walked her to the table, removed the liquor and bottles, and brought over pop. He set and held her hands.

"Since we gonna have a child, no sense in us not marrying."

She agreed. They got married before the baby came. A crowd came from the saloon and a few from church.

After the baby's birth, Cora began going to a sanctified church and became a Holy Roller. Later, she dragged her husband along. He thought she was trying to make up for the earthly way she had lived and was getting ready for the Lord. He didn't know if she really felt the Spirit, she acted like it. Sometimes she would get so carried away shouting she would bounce all over the place. The men liked watching her boobs jumping and her thighs showing when her dress rose. The women, of course, were jealous. Slowly she became less outrageous. She changed her manner of dress and shouted less. The congregation now accepted her as a settled woman. After a few months, she was pregnant again.

Craves strutted around the saloon, telling the boys he was gonna write as long as long as his pencil could but stopped eating barbecue and corn bread so he could cut back on his spelling.

Craves and Cora rode a two-seat, two-pedal bicycle, the ones popular at the turn of the century.

"Something's gonna happen that's gonna change the whole South," he said. "The Democrats are claiming state's rights. They done ran all the colored elected officials out of office with the Republicans."

Cora said, "That's gonna give them the right to handle us again like they want. We didn't get that book learning we should've. Let's make sure little Abraham and little Craves get it. Thank the Lord we're doing all right, but with that book learning, the children will be able to help themselves and do better."

Craves had a birthday party. His wife's children who had grown were there with some of Shirley's and Joe's from Ohio. Daisy, Tecumseh's wife, was there. He and Cherokee were still in the Philippines.

Daisy said, "I went to visit Happyness on the reservation. She is staying there until Cherokee returns. Her English is a lot better. Most of the Chiricahua are back in Arizona. They won't let the old man return. Everyone knew the old man was Geronimo. Geronimo asked to return to the land that he loved. He was told by President Teddy Roosevelt the land and people there don't want or miss him. After all those years, people in Arizona still feared the man. Cherokee had been with the general at the old man's last surrender. The Chiricahua, along with their scouts, were forced into exile in Alabama then Florida." He was then at Fort Sill Oklahoma. A prisoner of war with right to roam as he pleased.

The End

ACKNOWLEDGMENTS

Historical accounts of Native Americans came from *The Historical Atlas of Native Americans* by Ian Barnes, a book.

Substantial facts of how US troops behaved in the Philippines due to General Jocob Smith's infamous order.

The part of the Zorro-like figure, Frank Fagen, I happened upon while reading of the period on the internet. The imaginary was Chato a historical Chiricahua. Some information of the soldier during that period was obtained from the monthly, *Real West* magazine.

EPILOGUE

Buffalo soldiers were men formed by life experiences. From mainly ex–field hands with knowledge only of their surroundings, they developed into seasoned fighting soldiers organized into units where they demonstrated their abilities. On the Western frontier, they made friends and fought warring tribes. Each man did his best and hoped for a better future for themselves and their kind.

The soldiers became veterans of wars in Cuba, the Philippines, and World War I. Many of their war ventures were not covered by news correspondents who figured correctly. At the time, colored happenings had little interest. At the end of the 1900s going into the twenties, ex-slaves had been free for thirty-five years. The idea of the simple-minded blackface happy minstrel or buffoon was part of the American psyche.

By the time the immigrants arrived, they saw stereotypes in movies and people passing on the streets happy they were not molested like they had been in the South but still not accepted.

All former slaves were citizens. They all expected to be treated as such. Soldiers coming from the West or overseas had been engaged in combat or the job of pacifying new lands. They were returned by uniformed decision-makers to places where coloreds were openly called niggers. The local police made it a point to show them that even though they were in uniforms, they would only get the respect their kind received. The police, perplexed at the response of the soldiers, made explosive encounters inevitable. One happened in Brownsville, Texas, along the Rio Grande border. In 1906 the Twenty-Fifth Infantry got into a shoot-out with townspeople. Both sides had deaths. Thirteen soldiers were later executed and over 100 were dishonorably discharged.

In 1917 at Camp Logan in Houston, soldiers of the Twenty-Fourth Infantry were sent to guard the building of a camp for national guards being readied for the war in Europe. The town officials had gladly welcomed federal money the project would bring to the city. When they found out various companies coming would be colored, they expressed a desire that the soldiers be sent elsewhere. They did not want colored soldiers strutting around. It would be a bad example for the locals of the race who would follow their example and forget their place. Not take off their hats and bow to white people, or leave the sidewalk and get in the street when a white person passed.

After a riot that ensued, everyone agreed the police agitated it by calling the men out of their names daily. They had dragged a half-dressed local colored woman from her home. When a single colored soldier tried to intervene, he was pistol-whipped. When his corporal went to the police station, he was pistol-whipped and jailed. The soldiers marched on Houston. Fifteen white civilians and five soldiers were killed. Twenty-two were wounded. The court-martial that followed was the largest since the Irish Brigades during the Mexican War in 1848. There, the culprits were branded on the face as traitors or hung. This time no whites were brought to trial.

The proceedings were held in San Antonio at Fort Sam Houston Army Base. Thirteen were executed. They were not told until the day of the execution. Newspapers were uninformed until after it was over. Forty-one received life sentences. Over a hundred were dishonorably discharged and lost all benefits. After another trial, altogether nineteen were to be hung. Fifty-three received life. Slowly over the next twenty years with the help of the NAACP. All the ones in prison were released.

Findings in both sordid affairs are the following: In 1906, in Brownsville, President Theodore Roosevelt is 167 soldiers dishonorably discarded. In 1972, after an intensive investigation, the ruling was reversed by Congress and dismissed. The army made restitution to the soldiers' families.

After the Camp Logan convictions, President Woodrow Wilson pardoned ten of the convicted.

Some of the soldier were later sent to war in France still wanting the respect of the overall society. When they returned they were met with the bloodiest riots and race relations in the countries history. 1919 cities went up in flames in colored towns all over the North, South, and Mid West. Mostly blacks were killed many with uniforms on.

Printed in the USA
CPSIA information can be obtained
at www.ICGtesting.com
LVHW090457010324
773216LV00023B/234/J